*Here's what reviewers
are saying about*
TO HAVE AND TO HOLD

"At last a line that goes beyond the 'happily ever after' ending.... What really makes these books special is their view of marriage as an exciting, vibrant blossoming of love out of the courtship stage. Clichés such as the 'other woman' are avoided, as family backgrounds are beautifully interwoven with plot to create a very special romantic glow."
—Melinda Helfer, *Romantic Times*

"At last, a series of honest, convincing and delightfully reassuring stories about the joys of matrimonial love. Men and women who sometimes doubt that a happy marriage can be achieved should read these books."
—Vivien Jennings, *Boy Meets Girl*

"I am extremely impressed by the high quality of writing within this new line. Romance readers who have been screaming for stories of romance, sensuality, deep commitment and love will not want to miss this line. I feel that this line will become not only a favorite of mine but of the millions of romance readers."
—Terri Busch, *Heart Line*

"Do I look the same
as the day you married me?"
Glory asked in a whisper.

He screwed up one eye in thoughtful contemplation.
"No. You wore a dress that day, didn't you? White,
I believe?"

"You know what I mean." Glory gripped his thighs
and used them to push herself up his body until her
lips were poised above his. "Have I gained weight or
lost weight or...changed in any physical way?"

"You've gotten more lovable." His hands rested lightly
on the small of her back. "Physically, you're more
beautiful now than you were then. What about me?
Have I changed?"

Glory caressed his cheeks with the backs of her hands.
"You're lovely."

"Honey, for a writer you have a terrible vocabulary.
Men aren't cute or lovely."

"You are." Glory laughed softly as her love for him
swelled within her. "You defy description."

Dear Reader:

The event we've all been waiting for has finally arrived! The publishers of SECOND CHANCE AT LOVE are delighted to announce the arrival of TO HAVE AND TO HOLD. Here is the line of romances so many of you have been asking for. Here are the stories that take romance fiction into the thrilling new realm of married love.

TO HAVE AND TO HOLD is the first and only romance series that portrays the joys and heartaches of marriage. Its unique concept makes it significantly different from the other lines now available to you. It conforms to a standard of high quality set and maintained by SECOND CHANCE AT LOVE. And, of course, it offers all the compelling romance, exciting sensuality, and heartwarming entertainment you expect in your romance reading.

We think you'll love TO HAVE AND TO HOLD romances—and that you'll become the kind of loyal reader who is making SECOND CHANCE AT LOVE an ever-increasing success. Look for four TO HAVE AND TO HOLD romances in October and three each month thereafter, as well as six SECOND CHANCE AT LOVE romances each and every month. We hope you'll read and enjoy them all. And please keep your letters coming! Your opinion is of the utmost importance to us.

Warm wishes,

Ellen Edwards

Ellen Edwards
TO HAVE AND TO HOLD
The Berkley Publishing Group
200 Madison Avenue
New York, N.Y. 10016

To Have and to Hold ™

THEY SAID IT WOULDN'T LAST

ELAINE TUCKER

SECOND CHANCE AT LOVE
BOOK

For Peggy Fielding,
my own special "Penny"
who said it would *last.*

To Have and to Hold books are published by
The Berkley Publishing Group
200 Madison Avenue, New York, NY 10016

1

GLORY MATHERS WATCHED the flailing arms and wondered at the commotion. From her perch on the bench in the hotel lobby, she couldn't see the man very well. With a sigh she stood and craned her neck until she could.

"Isn't he handsome?"

Glory turned to see a cleaning lady, who was leaning against a broom, her tired eyes focused on Glory.

"Yes. He's nice-looking," Glory answered, swinging her gaze back to the man and his admirers.

"It's a sin for anyone to be that gorgeous."

Glory glanced at the woman again, taking in the lovesick expression. Should she tell her that the man put on his pants one leg at a time just like every other man? No, she decided. It would spoil the image she could see glowing in the other woman's eyes.

"Look at that smile! Looks like a toothpaste commercial, doesn't it?"

Glory nodded, mentally adding: Yes, and that smile cost $3,500. She had the dental bill to prove it.

"I hope his hair is real," the woman moaned. "When I heard that my favorite soap star wore a wig, I just died!"

Glory shifted her gaze to the man's lustrous hair. It's real, she thought. It may be thinning a little, but it's all his.

"I've seen all of his movies. Have you?"

Glory nodded. "Every last one of them."

"Which is your favorite?"

"Tie-Breaker," Glory answered automatically.

"Oh? My favorite is —"

"The Stick Man," Glory interrupted.

"Yes!" The woman looked at Glory in amazement. "How did you know that?"

Glory shrugged. "That's everyone's favorite."

The woman sighed and leaned heavily on the broom. "He's just so romantic. You know?"

Glory resisted the urge to inform her acquaintance that he wasn't any more romantic than any other red-blooded, thirty-eight-year-old American male.

"Aren't you going to get his autograph?"

Glory shook her head. "I have his autograph."

"I'm gonna get mine now. Bye." The woman took the broom with her and used it to part the human sea that surrounded the man. Glory watched her thrust a piece of paper under his nose.

He's got that "public" smile on, Glory thought as she watched the proceedings. She knew that by this time his cheek muscles were screaming for relief. Glory picked up her purse and attaché case and walked toward the throng of women. A camera crew was setting up bright lights, aiming them at him. He blinked.

Uh-oh, Glory thought with a smile. The tinted contact lenses his agent made him wear to enhance his already beautiful blue eyes were beginning to irritate him. She glanced around the lobby, wondering what was taking her children so long to purchase a bottle of aspirin in the hotel's gift shop. Three small figures caught her eye, and Glory grimaced when she saw that they were fussing with each other. Adam sent Damon sprawling, and Dani came to the rescue by kicking her older brother in the shin. When Adam retaliated by grabbing a handful of his sister's black curly hair, Glory hurried toward them as Dani's shriek filled the air.

"Stop it!" Glory clenched her teeth and pushed Adam to one side while she helped Damon to his feet. Adam pointed an accusing finger at his younger brother, who was red-faced and sobbing.

"He started it! Spank him!"

Glory drew a deep breath. "Adam, I didn't come over here to referee or dole out penalties. Where's the aspirin?"

Adam held out a crumpled sack, and she snatched it from his fingers.

"Where's my change?" She held out her hand, palm up.

"You said we could buy something!" Adam pinned her with an accusing glare.

"Yes," Glory conceded. "I said you could buy gum or candy—"

"Or something," Adam reminded her defensively.

"So? What did you buy, and where's my change?"

"We bought a poster. Here's your change." Adam dropped two quarters and three pennies into her palm.

"What?" Glory stared at the miserable sum. "What kind of poster costs three dollars?"

"It's an *E.T.* poster," Adam informed her. "It's real neat."

"*Real* neat," Damon agreed as he wiped his wet cheeks with his dimpled hands.

"Real neat," Glory echoed with a sneer that produced giggles from her offspring. "Well, now that everyone in the hotel knows we're here, let's go up to the room."

Adam grabbed the poster from Dani and sprinted ahead to the elevator. Dani started to wail but stopped abruptly when Glory sent her a killing glance.

"Adam!" Glory made her tone ominous as she reached the elevator and bent at the waist to caution her eldest eye-to-eye. "That's two. Three strikes and I'm gonna deck you. Got it?" She waited for his solemn nod. "Now give the poster to Dani and quit making a scene."

"But it's—" His gaze locked with Glory's, then he shrugged and handed the poster to his sister.

"Good." Glory ruffled his hair and straightened. "Press the 'up' button, please."

Adam whacked the button and looked back over his shoulder at the blaze of lights.

"Isn't Daddy coming with us?"

"No. He's playing movie star. He'll be up later," Glory answered as she waited for the elevator.

"Ugh!" Adam stuck out his tongue. "Boring."

"Those ladies are silly," Dani said with a frown as she watched the women elbow their way to the front of the crowd.

Glory looked over her shoulder at the movie star. Who is he? she wondered with an inner smile. Did she really sleep with that man? No, not *that* man. That man was so polite! Her husband was impatient. That man had a big, toothy smile. Her husband had a lip-stretching grin.

The movie star glanced up and caught Glory's eye. One dark eyebrow climbed his forehead in a gesture that was endearingly familiar to Glory. She waved at him before stepping into the elevator with the children.

When the elevator doors slid open, the children burst out like wild broncos. They dashed to the left; Glory turned to the right. As Glory made her way to the door marked 1422, she heard the sound of their footsteps stop suddenly before bounding back in her direction. The door was ajar, and Glory pushed it open for the children to precede her.

A bellhop was placing a huge vase of flowers on the

coffee table in the sitting room. He whirled, and his eyes widened when the children rushed past him to the bedroom. He looked at Glory, and she caught a flicker of disappointment in his eyes.

"Uh . . . Mrs. Wilson?"

"Ms. Mathers," she corrected.

"Pardon me?"

"Oh, never mind. Yes, I'm Mrs. Wilson."

"Well, I placed your luggage in the bedrooms."

"And where's my typewriter?" Glory asked as she tossed her purse and case into a nearby chair.

"Oh, it's with the other luggage."

"Thanks." Glory glanced at the change in her hand, then reached for her purse again. She found a dollar bill and extended it and the change toward the bellhop. "Here you go."

He looked at the tip as if Glory had handed him a salami sandwich. "Thank you, Mrs. Wilson. Welcome to Miami."

After he'd left, Glory investigated the various flower arrangements. The only name she recognized on the cards was Arnold Fletcher.

"Mom! Mom!"

She turned as Adam came rushing toward her. "Yes?"

"I want the bed by the window!" Adam tugged her hand.

"*I* want the bed by the window." Damon skidded to her side and tugged her other hand.

"I'm the oldest, so I get first choice!" Adam clutched one of her fingers and yanked.

"*I'm* the oldest, and you're breaking my finger," Glory interjected as she disengaged herself. "Unpack your things, and I'll assign the bunks later."

Adam looked at Damon and mouthed, "I'm gonna get the bed by the window."

With an inner smile, Glory tapped Adam on the shoulder and mouthed, "I'm gonna get your rear end."

Adam grinned and stomped back into the bedroom with Damon stumbling behind him. Glory dropped into the nearest chair and wondered why she'd insisted on having children.

She closed her eyes as the sounds of the youngsters drifted to her from the other room. Weariness infected her, and her headache was making itself known again, but she was too tired even to open the aspirin bottle. She remembered how traveling had been so adventurous and simple before the children.

But that was a sword that cut both ways, she reminded herself. Adam and Damon and Dani were marvelous company; there was never a dull moment with them around.

The scrape of a key being inserted into the lock opened her eyes, and she waited for the door to swing open. She hoped that he was alone.

". . . and, of course, tomorrow there's that television interview," Arnold said as he strode into the room.

"What's that? Some kind of local talking-heads program?" Wade glanced at Glory, then looked back at Arnold.

"Hi, Glory." Arnold smiled at her, then addressed Wade again. "Yeah. It airs during the noon hour."

Adam and Dani burst into the room, and Glory grinned when Adam, clutching a piece of hotel stationery, waved it at Wade. His voice was falsetto, a comic imitation of the female sex.

"Can I have your autograph?"

Dani giggled and hugged Wade's knees as Wade flashed Adam a withering glare.

"Okay, okay, smartie." Wade snatched the paper from his son and patted his daughter's head. "Hi, honey. Let go or I'm going to fall."

Dani released her father, then tilted her face up. "Kiss me!"

Grinning, Wade picked her up and planted a kiss on her cheek. "Where's Damon?"

"He won't leave the bedroom," Dani answered.

"Why not?"

"He's sitting on the bed by the window, and he won't budge."

"He's a creep," Adam grumbled as he examined the flowers.

"Have you unpacked your things?" Glory straightened in the chair, brushing aside her irritation at having Arnold insert himself into their lives, as usual.

"I'm too liddle to unpack," Dani said as Wade set her on her feet.

Glory pushed her shoulder-length brown hair back from her face. "You weren't too 'liddle' to pack, Dani," she reminded her daughter. "Now you kids get to it."

When the children had sullenly left the room, Wade and Arnold sat on the couch. Glory smiled as Wade massaged his cheeks, and Wade gave her a quizzical glance.

"Now you know how Miss America feels," she teased.

"You said it." Wade's blue eyes twinkled, and for a few moments a current of understanding passed between him and Glory before Arnold broke the charge.

"Here's your schedule, Wade." Arnold handed him several typed pages, then focused his small brown eyes on Glory. "Glory, are you going to the dinner tonight?"

Glory cautioned herself not to be so sensitive where Arnold was concerned, yet she couldn't help noticing his slight frown when she answered, "I thought I might. It sounds better than a Big Mac."

Arnold fidgeted. "But you're not taking the kids, right?"

Glory fixed Arnold with a cold stare. "Yes, we are."

Arnold's frown took on strength as he turned to Wade, dismissing Glory. "Do you think that's a good idea? I mean, the kids will be bored. They'll squirm around and take the spotlight from you."

Anger flashed through Glory, propelling her from the chair. She moved toward the bedroom, but she couldn't keep her acid remark from spilling forth. "Heaven forbid that anyone should steal his spotlight!"

Immediately she was contrite. As she helped her children unpack their clothes and hang them in the closet, she scolded herself for allowing Arnold to reduce her to planting immature barbs. It wasn't Arnold's fault. This *was* a business trip. Still, she couldn't douse her resentment. Arnold viewed her and the children as so much extra baggage.

He gaze fell on Damon, who was sitting in the middle of the bed by the window. His arms were folded across his chest, and he wore a stubborn expression. Loving awe consumed her. He looked so much like Wade! Damon had the same arched brows, the same blue eyes, the same black curly hair, the same full-lipped mouth and dimpled chin. He was a miniature Wade. She sat beside him on the bed and draped an arm around his small shoulders—shoulders that would someday be broad like his father's.

"I want this bed, Mom." Damon's lower lip jutted out.

Glory felt Adam's eyes on her, challenging her. She hugged Damon and kissed the top of his head. "Did you know that you look just like your Daddy?"

"Yeah. I want this bed, Mom."

"Mom, do we have any nails?"

Dani's question shattered Glory's train of thought. "Nails? Why?"

"We want to put up the poster."

Glory shook her head. "No. You can't put it up in

here. We'll have to wait until we get home, and you can hang it in your bedroom."

"Uh-uh!" The boys chorused, and Glory instantly realized the error she'd made.

"That poster belongs to all of us," Adam stated as he moved across the room to stand beside the bed. "She can't put it in *her* room."

Glory sighed. "So? Where are you going to hang it?"

"In the living room!" Damon turned his big blue eyes upward to find Glory's face.

"Yeah!" Adam nodded in agreement, obviously pleased with the suggestion.

"We can't put that poster in our living room," Glory admonished. "It . . . it wouldn't fit in."

"I've seen posters in other people's houses," Adam insisted as he sat on the bed, ignoring the warning glare Damon gave him.

In the corner of Glory's mind, she could see a poster hanging in a living room. It was of Spencer Tracy and Katharine Hepburn. Above their picture was the title *Pat and Mike*.

"Whatever happened to Spencer and Katharine?" she mused aloud as the vision became clearer in her mind.

"Huh?" Adam gave her a dumbfounded look, but Glory ignored him.

"Go finish unpacking," she ordered, gently pushing Adam from the bed. Her thoughts drifted, returning to the remembered poster. She could see herself staring at that poster, feeling warmth invade her as she recalled the movie.

"A match made in heaven, don't you think?" The words whispered past her lips as her mind back pedaled. She remembered turning away from the poster to confront the man who had spoken those words behind her. . . .

. . . and found herself staring at a patch of dark, curling

hair resting against a vee of tanned skin. Her gaze moved upward to find his face. He was handsome.

"Do you like Tracy and Hepburn?"

Glory turned away, thinking that his voice was that of an actor. She nodded and wished he would bother someone else. Actors were trouble.

"I think Tracy is the greatest actor who ever lived. He left no heirs."

She glanced at him again, noticing the cleft in his chin. It was just barely there; more like a dimple.

"I'm Wade Wilson."

She looked at him, her attention snared. *"You're* Wade Wilson?"

A black eyebrow lifted. "Yes. You're surprised?"

"Then this is your party." She winced, hearing the stupid statement.

"Yes. This is *my* party and *my* apartment. I guess that makes you *my* guest. Who are you?"

"I'm Glory Mathers, Trudy's roommate." She paused but got no reaction from him. "Trudy. The redhead in your drama class who's crazy about you."

The other eyebrow joined its mate. "Oh? I didn't know."

Glory groaned inwardly, not believing for a moment that he was unaware of Trudy's silent suffering. "Well, now you know." She stared at the poster and hoped he would move on.

"Are you an actress?"

"No, I'm a writer."

"Screenplays? Plays?"

"Novels and short stories."

"Have you had anything published?" he persisted, stepping closer to her.

Glory caught the scent of spicy aftershave, and she began to understand why her roommate was so attracted to this man. "I've had a couple of short stories published, and I just had a novel accepted."

"Wow!" He moved to stand beside her. "That's great. Aren't you excited?"

She lifted one shoulder. "Sure, I am."

"You have a funny way of showing it," he drawled.

Glory shot her eyes in his direction and was disconcerted when she found him studying her as if she were a script. She wondered what he could read in her face. "Why don't you ask Trudy for a date?" she blurted out, then looked away when she felt a blush creep into her cheeks.

"Why don't I ask *you* for a date?" he countered, his hand touching the small of her back.

"Because you hate rejection," Glory answered, determined to dissuade him.

"Oh? Why would you refuse?"

Glory decided to be honest with him. Why court disaster by attempting to let him down easy? "Because actors bore me to tears."

He seemed to take her caustic statement in stride. "Surely they can't be any more boring than writers."

Glory moved away from the touch of his hand on her back. She lifted her chin to fix him with a chilling stare. "Writers are more intelligent," she asserted. "They aren't in love with their own images."

His eyes darkened to a cobalt blue, and a muscle flexed in his jaw.

"Who was he? Do I know him?"

Glory looked away, her eyes staring blankly at the poster. "I don't know what you're talking about," she lied, while an image of Chuck Nation flashed into her mind. After Chuck, she'd vowed to steer clear of thespians.

"I'd like to blow out that torch you're still carrying, Glory Mathers." He leaned toward her, his fragrant breath fanning her cheek.

Glory pivoted from him and escaped into a group of people in the center of the room. She heard his low chuckle and wondered if Trudy knew what a flirt Wade Wilson could be?

Her remembrances faded as Damon squirmed beside her. Glory smiled at him and ran her fingers through his hair as one part of her mind clung to that party scene of so many years ago. It hadn't been the best of first impressions, she thought now. But she'd still been smarting from all of Chuck Nation's broken promises. She smiled. She'd loved to stick it to actors.

 2

"ARE YOU GOING to eat your roll?"

Glory looked at the overweight man seated beside her. He was some kind of Chamber of Commerce official, and his piglike eyes were focused on her dinner roll.

"No." Glory handed him the roll.

"Thanks." When he smiled, his eyes practically disappeared. "My weakness is bread." He bit into the roll, and the loose skin around his neck wiggled as he chewed.

Glory looked to her left where her children were seated. Damon was poking at the cardboardy green beans, Dani was shoveling mashed potatoes into her mouth, and Adam wasn't eating. His green eyes shifted from left to right as he surveyed the crowded room.

"Are those two little ones twins?"

Glory turned back to the man beside her and strangled her urge to reply, "No, those two little ones are triplets." She smiled instead and answered, "Yes."

"How old?"

"They're six."

"And the other boy?"

"He's eight."

"Wow!" The skin lifted around the man's eyes. "How long have you been married?"

Glory wanted to say, "Almost eight years," but again she quelled her mischievous streak. "We've been married ten years."

"That long?" He shook his head, and the last of Glory's dinner roll disappeared into his mouth.

Was ten years *that* long? Glory wondered. Maybe these people thought that ten years was a long time for a movie star to be married, but it wasn't a long time for a writer to be married.

Damon nudged her under the table. "Mom, we all need to go to the bathroom."

Glory sighed. "Okay." She shoved her chair back and led the way, all the while feeling the entire assemblage staring at her. They should be used to it by now, she thought. After all, this was her third trip in an hour-and-a-half.

Glory directed the boys to the men's room and went inside the ladies' room with Dani. She fished out her lipstick from her purse and touched up the mulberry color on her mouth while her daughter looked on.

"I wanna wear some," Dani announced.

Glory looked down at her. "Did you use the restroom?"

Dani shook her head. "I couldn't."

"I thought you needed to," Glory said as she smoothed the skirt of her burgundy evening dress.

"I just wanted to leave."

Glory smiled, knowing exactly how Dani felt. "You can't wear my lipstick."

"You let me once."

"At home, yes. Not in front of strangers."

"You wear it in front of strangers," Dani countered with stunning logic.

"I'm a grown-up." Glory winced, remembering how that all-purpose explanation had infuriated her when she was a child. She looked at her reflection in the mirror and tucked a few wayward strands of hair back into her neat chignon. She dreaded going back into the banquet room, but duty called.

Outside, the boys were waiting for them.

"Do we have to go back in there?" Adam pointed toward the room.

"Yes. They're going to serve dessert. You don't want to miss that, do you?" Glory attempted to weave an excited thread into her voice.

"If it tastes like the green beans, yeah," Damon grumbled.

Glory herded them toward the banquet hall, ignoring their feeble protests. She caught Wade's eyes, which held dark resentment within them. He was still angry at her for that caustic remark she'd made in front of Arnold. She rolled her eyes as she reseated herself at the head table. Wade Wilson could hold a grudge longer than anyone she'd ever known!

She noticed that the man beside her was watching her children, and she turned to see what had captured his interest. The children had resolutely pushed aside their dessert bowls of rice pudding.

"Aren't they going to eat their pudding?" the man asked, his tone hopeful.

"No." Glory shoved the pudding his way as the mayor of Miami took the rostrum to introduce the evening's guest of honor, Wade Wilson.

Wade backed up to Glory, and she unfastened his cummerbund.

"Do you want to go to that television program with me tomorrow morning?" he asked as he folded the sash.

Glory leaned back on the bed. "No. I'm taking the kids and my manuscript to the beach. I'll think of you."

"Thanks." He unbuttoned his frilly dress shirt and yanked the shirttails from his trousers. "You looked bored out of your mind during my speech."

"I wasn't," she objected. "I was plotting a novel."

Wade frowned. "Thanks, Glory."

"I've heard your speech." She shrugged and began taking down her hair.

"I always listen to your speeches," Wade grumbled as he removed his shirt, tossing it onto the bed.

"Wade, I listened to your speech." Glory sighed and ran her fingers through her hair, letting it fan out across her shoulders.

"Did it sound okay?"

"Of course it did." She smiled at his worried expression. "I wrote it, didn't I? Everything I write is great."

He had the good grace to grin at her as he unfastened his trousers. "Did you get the kids settled in?"

She nodded.

"Oh, by the way, who got the bed by the window?"

Glory laughed softly. "Damon. Adam was too tired to care. They were all exhausted and fell asleep as soon as their heads hit the pillows." She stood and stretched, trying to relieve the tension in her muscles. "I think I'll take a shower."

In the bathroom, she turned on the shower and stripped off her evening gown and underwear. The water temperature was just right, and she stood for several long minutes under the stinging spray. These affairs always left her limp and longing for her own bed in New York. Of course, they were necessary. Wade's new film had been shot in Miami, and the studio was determined to wring every cent it could out of this city. Tomorrow night they could go home.

For a few minutes, she reflected on Wade's leap to stardom and on the years he'd spent struggling to be noticed. What had happened to his dream of becoming a stage actor? she wondered. Had Hollywood destroyed that goal?

A sense of unrest stirred within her as she turned in slow circles under the shower spray. California was demanding more and more of them, and they were seeing

less and less of New York. For months she'd been waiting
for Wade to announce that they would have to make a
permanent move to California, and she knew she'd put
up a fight. She didn't like the California life-style. It
irritated her New York metabolism to sink into hot tubs
and spend her days jogging on the beach to keep up with
the Joneses.

You're being selfish.

The inner voice ripped through her mind, and Glory
turned off the shower. She stepped from the tiled stall
and began toweling herself. She wasn't being selfish,
she argued. She was being realistic. If Wade planted
himself in Southern California, he'd never go back to
New York and he'd never try to land a part on Broadway.
Hadn't that been his driving ambition? Had he changed
his career goal overnight?

"Glo!" A fist rapped on the bathroom door. "Can you
hurry it up? I'd like to shower before morning."

Glory pulled a face at the door as she wrapped the
bathsheet about her. She opened the door to find Wade
standing right outside.

"Finished—finally?"

Glory ignored his biting question and stepped around
him. She went to the double bed and pulled down the
bedspread. When she heard the shower running, she
slipped out of the bathsheet and into her peach-colored
negligee. With a sigh, she sat on the bed and plugged
in her hair dryer. The warm air blew her hair around her
head and into her mouth and eyes.

She *was* being selfish, she thought. This was important to him, and he needed her support. He'd been supportive last year when she'd left the kids with him and
embarked on a seven-city promotion tour for her last
novel. She shrugged and unplugged the hair dryer. Her
fingers slipped through her hair. It was still damp.

The bathroom door swung open, and Wade strode

toward her. "See? I showered in ten minutes. Why can't you do that?"

Glory let her gaze move slowly down his body, past the wide chest with its mat of dark hair, over his flat and firm stomach, to the nest of crisp hair below. She smiled, keeping her gaze pinned on that intimate part of his body. "I have more to wash," she teased.

He chuckled, bending to kiss her lips. "Smart-mouth," he murmured against her.

"It's the company I keep," she said, enjoying the sensation of his mouth rubbing against hers.

His knee came to rest at her side, and he pushed her back until she was lying on the bed.

"Tell me the truth," he murmured. "You still love me?"

Glory let her gaze rest lovingly on his dimpled chin. "Still," she assured him in a breathy whisper. "After all these years."

"What did I ever do to deserve you, Glo?"

"Just lucky, I guess." She shifted beneath him and felt him stir to life. "Let's get something straight between us," she said with a giggle, reciting a familiar catchphrase that had become a permanent part of their dialogue.

He laughed deep in his throat and kissed her ear. His tongue traced the curve of her earlobe with a featherlight touch.

"Stop!" Glory laughed and squirmed away from the tickling tip of his tongue. "Wade!"

"It's supposed to turn you on," he growled.

"I *was* turned on. Now I'm tickled."

His mouth moved to cover hers, smothering her mirth. Glory reached for him. When her hand circled him, she heard his swift intake of breath. He rolled to one side, and Glory looked down at her hand and smiled.

"Ten years, and I still think this is the most interesting thing about you," she whispered as her fingertips moved across the satiny skin.

"Thanks a lot, Glo," he said sardonically.

Glory laughed and stroked him, stoking his fires.

"Did you think my speech went okay—really?"

Glory frowned slightly, disturbed that he was bringing up such a dull subject at such a crucial time. "Yes. Fine."

He shifted his body and stilled her hand with his own. Glory looked up to watch his eyes darken in that way she'd come to know so well—that darkening that told her she was getting to him.

"You're a good writer, Glory." He smiled, the corners of his eyes crinkling. "What are you thinking about?"

"Us." Glory propped her head in one hand.

"What about us?"

"Do you feel like we've been married a long time, Wade?" She released him and traced the swirling colors in the sheet with her fingertip.

He tilted his head to one side and lifted that eyebrow. "Sometimes. But other times it seems as if we met each other just a few months ago. Remember Al's Drugstore?"

She nodded, the memory wrapping around her as her hand wrapped around Wade again. "What a classy place to begin such a wild and wonderful relationship," she said, her tone dripping with light sarcasm.

Wade shrugged. "It was about all I could afford, and besides, it *was* a special place . . .

". . . because you don't find places like this anymore."

Glory nodded and flicked a dead fly from the table. "You're right about that."

Wade looked at the fly on the floor and shrugged. "Did you tell Trudy you were meeting me?"

"No." Glory sipped from her glass of water. "But I'm

going to, and she's not going to like it. Why didn't you ask *her* out tonight? It would have made things so much simpler."

"Because I wanted to see you." His eyes bored into her, making her tense.

"Why?" Glory forced the one-word question past her dry throat.

"Why not?"

She wrinkled her brow as her thoughts turned to her roommate again. "This makes me feel guilty. Trudy really likes you a lot."

"Let's not talk about Trudy, okay?" Wade waited for Al to place two cups of coffee before them, then he continued, "Let's talk about us."

"Okay." Glory tested the coffee. It was strong. "What about us?" She stirred milk into her coffee and waited to see if anything floated to the top.

"Why don't you like me?"

His question startled her, but she feigned indifference. "I don't even know you."

"Well, let me start filling you in, since I do want you to like me. I live by instincts." He sipped the coffee, made a face, and pushed aside the cup. "When I met you at the party, my first instinct was to break down those walls you've constructed around yourself. I've even been pumping Trudy for information about you."

Glory sighed wearily. "That isn't nice."

"She seemed aware of my interest in you, and she hasn't seemed to mind," he said, sincerity written on his face. "There's nothing between me and Trudy. We're just friends—and we're not even close friends."

"But she likes you!"

Wade made a helpless gesture. "I can't help that any more than I can help wanting you," he said quietly.

"Wanting me?"

"Yes."

Glory looked away from his attractive blue eyes even as one part of her heart suddenly blossomed. She grimly reminded herself that this man was an actor and that she'd had her fill of those. But the tingling sensation continued to flower. She hadn't forgotten meeting him either, and she'd glowed inwardly when Trudy had told her that Wade asked about her daily. Yet there was something dangerous about Wade Wilson. Something, but what? His kindness. Glory nodded to herself. Yes, that kindness she saw in his eyes. Even his concern that he was helpless to avoid hurting Trudy. Kindness in an actor. Lord, that was a dangerous combination! She'd thought he was just another self-centered performer, but he was different. And he wasn't bad to look at either.

"Would you like to go to my apartment and make love?"

Glory lifted her gaze to his again, thinking he would be smiling, but he wasn't. "You've got to be kidding," she accused.

"I'm not." His hand moved across the table to find hers. "Do you want to?"

"Hardly." She was sorely disappointed. Why did men always put their feet into it? Why couldn't they be romantic? Oh, no. They just barged right in, blurting out things that no woman in her right mind was ready to hear. She squared her shoulders, mentally thanking him for slapping her back into the real world. "I'm not interested in you, Wade Wilson. I thought I made that clear when we met at the party." She slid from the booth and walked quickly to the door. Wade just as quickly followed her, and his fingers curled around her upper arm, stopping her just shy of the screened door. His eyes were midnight blue.

"What's wrong, Glory? I know you're attracted to me

or you wouldn't have met me here tonight. Is it just because I'm an actor? Are you going to hold that against me?"

Glory wrenched her arm from his grasp as fury blazed within her. "I don't go to bed with perfect strangers . . . especially after a date for a lousy cup of coffee in a first-rate dump!" She opened the door and stepped out into a sheet of rain. Car lights bounced off the slick concrete as she waved frantically at an approaching taxi.

Inside the cab, she shook the raindrops from her shirt and jeans. Trudy was crazy! What did she see in that egomaniac?

And what possessed me to meet him tonight? Glory asked herself. An ironic smile touched her lips. She knew perfectly well why she had agreed to meet him. She hadn't been able to get him out of her mind, although she'd tried for weeks. What with Trudy bringing home reports of how he kept asking about her, and his persistently cropping up in her recent unusually erotic nightly dreams, escape seemed impossible. Even when he'd been cocky enough to ask her to sleep with him, Glory had to admit there'd been a tingle of desire in the pit of her stomach at the prospect.

If only he'd wooed her a little!

Glory heaved a frustrated sigh. Obviously he wasn't accustomed to having to woo females. She shrugged off a sudden feeling of regret.

Once back at the apartment she shared with Trudy, she slipped quietly into bed, relieved when Trudy showed no signs of awakening. She'd have to tell her roommate about this tomorrow, and it wouldn't be easy to explain. The telephone bell splintered the silence, and Glory snatched up the receiver.

"Hello?" Her voice was breathless.

"I'm sorry, Glory. So sorry."

The line went dead, and Glory stared at the receiver

for a moment before replacing it in the cradle. Trudy stirred, and Glory snuggled farther under the sheet...

Wade's mouth was warm against the side of her neck, drawing her back to the present. His hands covered her breasts as he shifted his weight to cover her.

"You smell so good," he said, nuzzling her throat. "You always have smelled delicious." His tongue traced a moist path to her collarbone.

Glory wrapped her arms about his neck, arching her body to join his. He began chanting her name, the chant quickening with his thrusts.

Glory smiled. She loved the sound of his voice.

3

GLORY STARED AT the blank piece of typing paper in her electric typewriter. How could she expect to work when Wade had dropped a bombshell this morning?

Her gaze wandered around her office. She'd spent two years getting this office in the apartment just right. Hours had been spent refinishing her desk. Days had slipped by when she'd wallpapered the room in a pattern of vivid yellows and oranges. Weeks had disappeared as she'd carefully arranged her storehouse of books into the custom-made bookcases. She could work here. She was comfortable here. Didn't Wade understand that? Didn't he understand that she couldn't work in California?

"Hi! It's just me."

Glory whirled to face her mother, and the words "I'm working!" fell automatically from her lips. She felt a stab of regret as she watched her mother's smile fade.

"That's some greeting." Her mother held out a Tupperware container. "I brought you some macaroons."

With a frustrated sigh, Glory leaned back in her chair and fixed an apologetic smile on her lips. "Hello, Mother. I thought you had some kind of meeting today."

Her mother sat down in the chair beside Glory's desk. "I'm in between meetings. I just finished a Gray Panthers meeting, and I'm on my way to an aerobics class. How was Miami?"

"Hot." Glory massaged her neck muscles with one hand. "I'm glad to be home."

"Where's Wade?"

"He's at Stan Fedderman's office signing a contract. We're going to California. Wade's doing another movie." A movement caught Glory's eye, and she looked past her mother to find Peaches standing in the doorway. Her long, skinny arms crossed over her flat chest, and her black eyes flitted from Glory's mother to Glory.

"I told her you was working, but she wouldn't listen," Peaches announced.

"It's okay," Glory said quickly. "Where are the kids?"

"Watching something on TV."

"Okay." Glory looked back at her mother, but Peaches stood scuffing her shoes against the carpet. Glory acknowledged the body language. "Is something wrong, Peaches?"

Peaches frowned, bringing lines to her dark face. "I couldn't help but hear you and Mister Wade fussing this morning. Are you moving to California for good, or what?"

Glory pinched the bridge of her nose between her forefinger and thumb, feeling her mother's worried eyes bore into her. "Peaches, we'll talk about this later, okay? Not now."

Peaches shrugged. "I just wanted to know what's going to happen to me."

"Later." Glory gave her a pointed glare, and the woman backed from the room, closing the door behind her.

"Did you and Wade have a fight?" Glory's mother leaned forward, placing a hand on her daughter's forearm.

"Yes." Glory sighed, meeting her mother's eyes. "I don't want to move to California."

Her mother's green eyes widened, and she leaned back in her chair. "He wants to move there permanently?"

"Yes, he's already bought the house in Malibu that we've been renting. That's what I'm so mad about." Glory shook her head, unable to let the lie stand between her and her mother. "No, that's not true. I don't like Hollywood. I can't work there. My agent and publisher are here."

"You told me once that you can work anywhere." Her mother's voice was soft, hesitant.

"Mother, all my friends are here," Glory said, trying to make her mother understand. "Writer friends, I mean. They're so important to me. I can have lunch with them, and we discuss book ideas and problems that I can't discuss with other people. And then there's Penny. Any time I need her, she's just a ten-minute taxi drive away. I'm so . . . so shut off from everything and everyone in California."

"There's always the telephone, Glory. You can call your friends and Penny."

When Glory didn't respond, her mother opened the container she'd brought and plucked out a macaroon.

"Where in the world did you ever find Peaches?"

Glory smiled, shrugging off her feelings of desperation for the moment. "I advertised for a maid in *The New York Review of Books,* and Peaches answered it."

"I didn't know they let you advertise for stuff like that in the *Review.*"

Glory laughed. "They don't usually, but they made an exception after I explained that I needed a maid who understood a writer's personality. I like Peaches. She's an original."

"She's a grouch. I think she hates me." A petulant look crossed her face.

"No, Mother. She just has orders to keep people out of here when I'm working."

"What are you working on?" Her mother looked at the white sheet of typing paper in the machine.

"I'm trying to finish a magazine article," Glory said, staring numbly at the blank paper. "I have to mail it in tomorrow."

"And this argument you had with Wade has you all stirred up, right?" Her mother bit into the macaroon.

"Right." Glory ripped the sheet of paper from the typewriter and tossed it into the tray beside the machine. "I guess I'm being unreasonable."

"Why don't you try talking to Wade instead of yelling at him?"

Glory's gaze whipped to her mother's face. "Are you taking his side already?"

"I'm not taking sides." Her mother brushed crumbs from her linen skirt. "I'm making a suggestion. Glory, this is a career move for him. He's spent years trying to break into show business. Don't erect barriers now."

"But what about *my* career?" Glory threw up her hands, halting her mother's words. "I know that I said I could work anywhere, but that was before I saw California."

"Glory," her mother scolded gently. "California isn't the real problem, is it?"

"No. Maybe we're just going through our first rough spot," Glory mused quietly. "I mean, we've been married ten years and..." She let the words trail into nothing, then placed her hands on her typewriter. "I've got to get back to work, Mother."

"What's the name of this new picture Wade's doing?" Her mother took another macaroon from the container.

"Twisting Turns. It's about a woman race-car driver and her manager/husband. Fiona Larkin co-stars."

"Isn't she in television?"

Glory nodded. "Yes, she was. Her series was cancelled. Remember? She was in 'The Fly Girls.'"

Her mother nodded. "Oh, yes. I hated that show. All the women acted like nitwits."

"Amen!" Glory shook herself. She didn't have time

to shoot the bull with her mother. There was the article to finish and then dinner... "Mother, I really have—"

"I'm home!"

Her mother's face brightened. "It's Wade! We're in here, Wade!"

Wade walked into the study, his eyes examining the sign that swung on the doorknob. "'Writer At Work. Do Not Enter,'" he read aloud. He looked at Glory. "Where'd you get that?"

"Penny gave it to me. She said that after she divorced Fred, she didn't need it anymore."

"Clever." He touched the sign, sending it swaying on its black string. "Hello, Edna-love. I thought you had some meetings today."

Edna Mathers nodded and tapped the Tupperware. "I brought some macaroons. Have one. I hear you're moving to California."

Wade's blue eyes moved to find Glory's. "Well, it looks that way, Edna."

Glory swallowed the bitter words that filled her throat. "Wade, will you watch the kids? I've got to finish this article."

"Sure, honey. Edna, can you stay for dinner?"

"No. I've got to go to my aerobics class." Edna stood and kissed Glory's cheek. "When are you heading for Tinsel Town?"

"Three weeks," Wade answered quickly.

Glory winced at the news. "Three weeks. Great."

"Well, we'll have to get together before you leave," Edna said, kissing Wade on the chin, then moving toward the door. "Your dad would like to see you and the kids."

"Name the night, and we'll be there," Glory said.

"I'll call you, sweetie."

Glory watched Wade escort her mother to the front door, then she turned back to the typewriter. Three weeks! Why so soon? Why hadn't he told her that this morning?

The study door inched open farther, and Damon peeked in.

"Damon, can't you read that sign?" Glory asked.

"Nope."

She glared at him, then sighed. "You know what it says."

"Grandmom said you had some macaroons in here."

Glory nodded, pointing to the pale pink container. "Here, take them and leave, please."

"Okay." His voice was tiny, and he scurried across the room, grabbed the macaroons, and made his escape. At the door he stopped and looked back at her. "Is Daddy in charge now?"

"Yes. I'm out to lunch."

"Okay. I'll tell Adam and Dani." He hurried out, slamming the door.

Glory placed her fingers on the typewriter keys, then realized she didn't have any paper rolled into the machine. Wearily she repositioned the blank page, then stared moodily at the picture of Wade that sat on one corner of her desk. Why couldn't he have waited until after she'd finished the article before he announced they were moving? He just didn't understand how much she needed to be in her own study in her own apartment. No one seemed to understand.

Tipping her head to one side, Glory sensed a feeling of déjà vu. Hadn't she lectured someone on the importance of writing before? She burrowed through her mind, trying to dig up the root of memory. A rejection slip! Yes, that was it. She could see it in her mind. A piece of pink paper trembling in her hands. Pink like Mother's Tupperware bowl. There was a wet spot on it. Oh, yes! She remembered now. She'd been crying, and Trudy was looking at her with a mixture of sympathy and confusion. She'd mumbled something about . . . about . . .

* * *

". . . going to pieces over it! Someone else will buy your novel. Grab hold of yourself, Glory."

"Trudy!" Glory waved the slip of paper in Trudy's face. "These creeps told me they'd buy my book, and now they're rejecting it unless I help finance the publishing costs! Don't you understand?"

"Yes, I understand, but it's a good novel. Send it someplace else."

Glory collapsed into a bean-bag chair. "I've told everyone I know that my novel's been accepted. Now I'll have to tell them it's not true." She crumpled the piece of paper into a ball and threw it against the wall.

"Look." Trudy knelt beside her, placing a comforting hand on her shoulder. "I know what you're going through. It's just like when I audition for a part and they tell me they'll call me, but they don't."

"It's nothing like that." A fresh supply of tears stung her eyes. "Don't compare acting to writing. They're totally different."

Trudy's expression hardened. "Will you get off your high horse? Rejection is rejection! I don't care if it's writing or acting or . . . your getting Wade instead of my getting him!"

Glory flinched from the verbal blade and studied Trudy for a moment, watching resentment pinch her face.

"Trudy, I don't have Wade. I haven't seen him since that night in the café, and that was months ago. How many times do I have to tell you that?"

A haughty expression covered Trudy's round face. "I was just using him as an example."

"It's a poor example."

"He doesn't talk to me much anymore," Trudy said, her mouth forming a pout. "He said something about taking lessons from a different coach the other day, and—"

"For heaven's sake!" Glory scrambled from the bean-bag chair. "Who cares about Wade Wilson? I've just received a rejection slip, my whole world is manure, and you're talking about a conceited, egotistical louse!"

"He is not!" Trudy's face flamed. "You like him. I know you do."

"You're the one making a fool of yourself over him, not me."

"I love him." Trudy stomped toward the bedroom.

"You love him?" Glory asked in disbelief.

Trudy stopped and stared at the carpet for a few seconds before turning back to Glory. Mischief danced in her brown eyes. "I'd love to get him in the sack . . . just once!"

Glory nodded. "That sounds more like it, my friend."

Trudy shoved her hands into her jean pockets and rocked back and forth on the soles of her feet. "I'm sorry, Glory. It just ticks me off that I want him, he wants you, and you don't care. It's not fair."

"And it's not my fault," Glory added. "Trudy, you know I'd never do anything to hurt you."

"I know." Trudy stared at her toes for a moment before lifting her gaze to Glory's. "I wouldn't be hurt if you started seeing him. I think we should keep him in the family." She dimpled, then added, "And I'm sorry about your novel."

Tears smarted in her eyes again, and Glory blinked, trying to hold onto a shred of composure. "I guess I'll live."

"Sure you will." Trudy's smile was positive. "It'll sell, and you'll show them all!" She pivoted and started for the bedroom again. "If I were you, I'd call Wade and let him come over to comfort me. I bet he's good at that."

Glory watched her roommate disappear into the bedroom, marveling at Trudy's one-track mind . . .

* * *

"Glory? Hey, Glo?"

Glory jumped and swung her gaze around to confront Wade, who stood in the threshold of the study. "What?"

"Can I interrupt a minute?" He stepped into the room and closed the door, not waiting for her permission. "I'd like to talk to you about this California thing."

"Okay. I was just thinking about Trudy." Glory pushed back her chair and crossed her legs, Indian fashion.

"Trudy?" Wade smiled. "Have you heard from her since she got married?"

"Yes. She and Lance have settled on a farm in Iowa. She said she feels right at home playing to a bunch of turkeys."

Wade chuckled as he sprawled on the low, two-cushioned couch. He laced his fingers together and stared at his wedding band. "Let's make a deal, partner."

Glory stiffened as if preparing to do battle. "Okay. Let's hear the deal."

"We'll move to California—temporarily. After the film is completed, we'll discuss it and decide together whether or not to make a permanent move." He tore his gaze from his wedding band to look at her. "How does that strike you?"

"It's better than the first ultimatum." Glory untangled her legs and went to sit beside him. She linked her arm in his and leaned her cheek against his shoulder. "I love New York City, Wade. Don't you?"

"I can't find work here, Glory."

She closed her eyes. "You haven't tried since you made it big. Things have changed now."

"I'm a film actor. That doesn't guarantee a part on Broadway." He covered her hand where it rested on his bicep. "We should wrap the film within three months."

"Okay, California here we come—for now." Glory lifted her head and pressed a kiss to his cheek. "Thanks for compromising."

"A sense of fair play is one of my best qualities," he said with a grin. "You're so lucky to have me."

Glory smiled. She loved his humility.

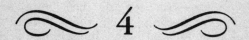

4

FROM HER VANTAGE point near the restaurant's entrance, Glory glimpsed the sleeve of a colorful caftan.

She stood on tiptoe to peer around the taller pedestrians so that she could see Penny. Glory smiled as she watched Penny approach her. The caftan swished around Penny's legs, and she held her head high in that proud way that was so attractive.

"Hi, Penny."

Penny enveloped Glory in a warm embrace, and her pixie face broke into a smile. "How was Miami? Did you get some work done?"

"Not as much as I'd planned," Glory admitted as she entered the restaurant and wove through the tables to one located near the back of the crowded room. "But I finished that magazine article and sent it off."

"Did Wade stick you with the kids in Miami?" Disgust drew Penny's brow together.

"Well, it was *his* business trip," Glory reminded her. "I wrote a few chapters."

"That's pretty good, I guess." Penny's purse slid from her lap, and a man walking past stooped to retrieve it. Penny flashed him a smile that seemed to lift the tip of her pug nose. "How very kind of you."

The man blushed under Penny's warmth and muttered something appropriate. He tore his gaze from Penny's face and stumbled toward his table.

"Penny, you're marvelous." Glory laughed at her literary agent's innocent expression. "How could old Fred give you up?"

A bitter smile captured Penny's mouth. "Fred wanted his pretty young mistress." The bitterness dissipated and was replaced by a confident expression. "It was the best thing that ever happened to me, Glory. I'm free to be creative again. No more trying to be Fred's little woman." Penny studied the menu for a few moments, then added in a hushed voice, "I've met the most darling man, Glory."

"Oh?" Glory leaned forward, eager for Penny's expansion.

"Yes." Penny's brown eyes twinkled. "He's a tall, *tall* Texan, complete with a ten-gallon hat. And you should see his pistol!"

Laughter bubbled from Glory's throat as she waited for the next installment.

"We have an understanding," Penny continued in a conspiratorial tone. "We don't clutter up each other's lives. We just enjoy a few stolen hours here and there. It's the only way to have a man, Glory. I'm never going to take in another man I have to raise. Never!"

The waiter approached the table, and Glory and Penny ordered. Through her lashes Glory examined Penny—her friend, editor, and agent. She wondered about her age. Forty? Fifty? With Penny it was impossible to determine—and somehow unimportant. She was the type of woman who was and should be ageless.

"You sound a little turned off to men, Penny," Glory suggested when the waiter had moved to the next table.

"Oh, no!" Penny looked shocked. "They're lovely. I just want them to remain in their place. You see, I've provided a corner of my life for them." She leaned closer to Glory, pressing her point. "You should never allow a man to become more important than your writing, Glory."

Glory nodded, wondering if she should tell Penny that Wade and the children were more important to her than her writing. No, she decided. She didn't want to spoil their lunch.

"How's Wade?"

"He's fine. He's signed for another picture, but I don't think he's happy about it."

"He doesn't like the superstar scene?"

Glory gave Penny a thoughtful look. "You see right through people, don't you?" She shook her head, bewildered. "Wade's wrestling with himself right now. He can't decide if he should take the Hollywood money and run, or set his sights on the stage again. I wish he'd try Broadway. I'm afraid he'll keep doing films and forget about his dream to act before live audiences."

"You should let *him* worry about his career, and you should worry about yours. I'm waiting for that novel, Glory. I think Wade's getting in your way." Penny held up a hand to stop Glory's protest. "I know. He's a marvelous-looking man. Believe me, I'd have trouble staying out of bed, too. But you need to finish that novel."

"Penny, Wade is very supportive."

Penny smiled as the waiter served her a club sandwich and placed a chicken salad sandwich before Glory. When the waiter was out of earshot, Penny directed her gaze to Glory again. "I know he's supportive. I just don't want you to get so involved in his success that you forget about yours."

Glory took a bite of her sandwich. Should she tell Penny that Wade's success was keeping her up nights? Should she confide her recent soul-searching? No. She wasn't ready to talk about it. Just thinking about it frightened her. Sometimes she felt as if Wade was slipping away from her.

"How far are you on the novel?"

Glory sipped her wine. "About halfway, I guess."

"Good. Send me what you've finished. I can get started on it."

Glory smiled, awed by Penny's continuous drive. Penny was to writing what Oral Roberts was to prime-time religion: powers unto themselves. "Penny, you seem to be adjusting just fine to the single life."

Penny nodded. "I could kick myself for the years I wasted on Fred. I'm writing again, and I'd forgotten how much fun it could be. You know, I'm not taking any money from him."

Glory almost choked on her food. "What? Why not?"

"I don't want it." Penny lifted her chin. "He can spend it on his mistress. I've washed my hands of him—entirely."

Glory sipped her wine, impressed by Penny's un-sinkable spirit. She waited for Penny to finish her lunch.

"So, you'll spend the summer in California?" Penny asked, pushing aside her plate.

"Yes." Glory sighed, feeling depression nudge her peaceful mood. "We're staying in Malibu again. It's a nice place to write," she lied.

"I'm glad. You've slowed up this past year."

"I know." Glory finished her wine. "But when your husband is nominated for an Academy Award and every-body and his dog wants him for a personal appearance, it cuts into your time."

"That's *his* time, not yours."

A helpless feeling wormed its way into Glory, and she looked to Penny for support. "Penny, I want to be with him. Try to understand. We've both worked and struggled to get to this point. I'm proud of him. Don't you see?"

Some of that stubborn spirit left Penny's face, and she lowered her chin a fraction. "Who can blame you?

I remember all those years when you supported him—"

"And he was proud of me and still is," Glory hurried to interject.

"Yes, I know. He really is a lovely man." Penny fingered her necklace of exotic beads, arranging them so that they fell between her ample breasts.

"Have you lost weight?" Glory tried to glimpse Penny's form, which was concealed by the caftan.

"Heavens, no." Penny frowned. "You know writers. They sit on their rears all day and let everything they eat turn to flab. You're the exception, but your day's coming." Her eyes sparkled. "The only exercise I get is pushing a pencil and hitting typewriter keys."

Glory nodded. "If it weren't for the kids, I might have a problem. They keep me running." Glory reached for her purse. "I'll get this one." She pulled some bills from her wallet and laid them on the tray. "Business luncheon, Uncle Sam, dear."

Penny laughed and moved with Glory toward the exit. Outside, Glory hugged Penny and felt depressed at having to leave her and New York for the eternal facade of Hollywood. She watched Penny walk away, and she laughed to herself at the image her literary agent projected. Penny looked like a woman who thought she was better than most people and knew she was better than some.

Glory turned and strolled down the busy sidewalk. A taxi slowed and cruised beside her, but she shook her head, and the driver accelerated past her. Her attention was captured by the couple in front of her. Arms entwined, they seemed lost in each other. The couple entered a hamburger joint, and Glory paused to look through the cloudy windows.

Something about the place seemed familiar. She watched a waiter scurry to the couple. The waiter was young, and Glory wondered if he was an aspiring actor.

He turned, and his eyes found hers. He smiled, and Glory smiled back . . .

. . . before she recognized him. Her lips formed his name. "Wade Wilson." He nodded, motioning for her to come inside the café.

For a moment, she started to shake her head, but the unexpected joy of actually seeing him in the flesh overruled the impulse.

Wade Wilson! Seeing him again made her realize how often she'd thought of him over the past few months. She'd furtively searched reviews of Off-Broadway plays for his name. She'd oh-so-casually asked her few theatrical acquaintances if they'd seen him around. Finally she'd decided he must have joined a traveling company. It wasn't like her to dwell on a man, but somehow Wade Wilson had imprinted himself on her memory. He made her feel as if she were missing something—him.

And here he was, waving her into the café, his eyes that same feverish blue she remembered so well.

"What in the world are you doing here?" She surveyed his jeans, T-shirt, and white apron.

"I'm trying to make a living and not doing a very good job of it." He looked over his shoulder. "Sit in that last booth, and I'll join you for a cup of coffee."

Again she started to decline, but curiosity and her grudging attraction to the man got the best of her. She walked to the appointed booth and slid into her seat. She watched Wade pour coffee into two mugs, then he joined her.

"How's Trudy doing?"

"Trudy is touring with a repertory company. I assumed you were doing the same."

Frustration edged its way into his eyes. "I wish. I haven't been able to find any theater work." He blew at the rim of his cup, and Glory noticed how wide and full his lips were.

She found herself staring at him, moving her gaze from his mouth to his eyes. Envy stayed her gaze, and she found herself wishing she had his thick, dark lashes. The lashes lifted, and two blue eyes focused on her.

"Where are you living?"

"At the same place. How about you?"

He frowned. "I'm staying at the Y."

"You're kidding. That sounds grim."

"It is."

A burly man behind the counter called to Wade, who grimaced. "I've got to get back to work. It was nice seeing you again, Glory." He stood and offered his hand.

Glory looked at his hand, long-fingered and well-shaped. "You can stay with me, Wade," she said, much to her surprise.

"What?"

She lifted her gaze to see his shocked expression. "You can stay at my place." She swallowed, wondering where she'd found this new, brave Glory. "Trudy's room is just sitting there. You can use it until your luck breaks."

He tipped his head to one side and quirked an eyebrow. "Why are you doing this?"

"Because I know how terrible it is to be broke. Do you want the room or not?"

"Glory, I can't pay—"

"If I was looking for a Sugar Daddy, I wouldn't pick you, Wilson," she interrupted with a smile.

His mouth curved into a tantalizing grin. "I get off work at seven. Is that okay?"

"That's fine with me."

"Thanks, Glory. You've saved my life." He pivoted and walked to the burly man.

Several hours later he arrived at the apartment as promised and stowed his belongings in the extra bedroom. After dinner he sprawled in the chair near the fireplace, and Glory curled up on the couch, feeling uneasy and hating him for being so comfortable in her home while she squirmed.

"Thanks for dinner. I was starved."

She tried to smile but felt the failure on her lips. "You're welcome. I guess you work pretty hard at that coffee shop."

"Yes, especially during the lunch hour and after school." He stretched his legs in front of him. "I wish I could find a theater job."

"Have you ever had a theater job?"

He looked at her as if she were insane. "Sure. I've played summer stock, and I was in a repertory troupe after I graduated from Syracuse."

"You went to college?"

He arched a dark brow. "Yes. I'm not as dumb as I look. I graduated and received a fellowship grant to apprentice with the Royal Shakespeare Company in England. After that, I toured the States and then entered the academy."

Glory was surprised and impressed. What had made her think that this man was empty-headed? Why hadn't she noticed the intelligence in his eyes before? Had his handsome features blinded her to his more enviable traits?

"I love Shakespeare," Wade said, straightening in the chair and clasping his hands behind his neck. "How I envy people who can create such characters. Such drama!" His voice and eyes were dreamy. "People like you."

Glory laughed. "Shakespeare must be turning over in his grave at that comparison."

He smiled and shifted positions, resting his elbows on his knees and hooking her with a bright blue stare. "Why don't you like actors?"

The turn of conversation threw her for a moment, and she squirmed again, burrowing her body deeper into the cushions. "I . . . I don't know. I find them conceited."

"You must have met some losers. Most of the actors I know are intelligent and dedicated to their craft—not to their egos." The intense gaze left her to focus on the empty fireplace.

Glory swallowed and felt the uneasiness again. Why was she so nervous? This was a bad idea. This roommate thing wasn't going to work. She couldn't sleep with him here. She probably wouldn't even be able to work with him here.

"I really loved those days with the company in England," Wade mused aloud. "The people were so professional—and the country!" His feverish gaze captured her again. "Have you ever been there?"

"No." It seemed as if a current of excitement was reaching across the room to her. She leaned back against the couch to try to break the charge.

"You'll have to visit it someday. It's got a lot to offer, especially to a writer."

She searched her mind for something to say to him. Something that would ease the nagging feeling in the pit of her stomach. "Uh . . . you miss that time in England, don't you?" Glory cringed and wanted to bite her tongue when she saw a flicker of amusement enter his eyes. Did he know how uncomfortable she was? She tried again. "I mean, you'd like to be there right now, wouldn't you?"

A slow smile curved his mouth. "No, I don't believe in living in the past. I like the here and now." That arched eyebrow slid down to join the other, forming a dark bridge above blue eyes. "So why don't you come here. Now," he whispered.

Glory sucked in her breath and stared at him. She prayed for courage. She prayed for the telephone to ring or the doorbell to chime. Did he expect her to make the first move? She couldn't! Dammit, she did want him, yes, but why didn't he kiss her or something?

Wade sighed and shook his head. "This isn't going to work, Glory."

"What?" She pulled her lower lip between her teeth, thinking that she sounded like an imbecile.

"I thought I could live here with you, but it's stupid. I don't think I'd be too good at a platonic relationship with you."

The yellow streak down her back began to fade as necessity tore through her. He was going to leave, and she couldn't let him do that. She'd found him—finally!

"Do you ever think of me?" she asked in a whisper.

He seemed startled for a moment. "No more than five or six times a day. Why?"

She smiled and stood, straightening her spine and lifting her chin. She'd gotten under his skin, too! That was what she needed to know. A wary expression flitted across his face as she crossed to sit in his lap, curling her fingers in the hair on the back of his head. So he *had* been baiting her! Well, she'd beaten him at his own game.

He narrowed his eyes. "Now, let me get this straight..."

Glory looked at his mouth and thought how wonderfully close it was to hers. As his lips touched hers, she sighed in relief. His lips moved, insistent, impatient. Glory pulled away and smiled.

"Now do I make myself clear?"

He nuzzled her neck. "To quote a friend, 'I take thee at thy word.'"

Glory smiled, loving the way his hands seemed to know her...

An ambulance siren blared behind her, and Glory jumped and whirled from her sightless view of the café. She shook herself mentally, disengaging the last clinging threads of her reminiscence. On impulse, she decided to visit the Statue of Liberty. They didn't have such things in California, she thought with a twinge of nostalgia. So many memories were planted here. So many places made her remember Wade and those early, thin-iced days when they'd stripped away the layers one by one to find each other.

Glory smiled. She loved New York and the man she'd found here.

5

"MOM, WHY ARE these daisies stuck all over this window?" Adam traced one decal with his fingertip.

Glory straightened from loading the dishes into the dishwasher to look at him. "To keep you from running through the glass."

He looked insulted. "I'm not *that* dumb."

Glory laughed softly. "Is Peaches out there with Dani and Damon?"

"Yeah. They're building another sand castle." He looked over his shoulder. "See you later, Mom." He opened the sliding door, letting the furious sound of the ocean into the room, then closed it behind him.

Glory stood by the doors and watched the beach shimmer in the heat. Peaches was constructing a turret on the castle the children were building. Once again, Glory was thankful that Peaches had decided to come with them to California. She was so good with the kids and so understanding of Glory's need to work alone. Glory squinted, watching the foam line of the ocean on the sand. Her attention was arrested by a stunning bikini-clad young woman. Her golden body was sleek and slender, and her hair was an unbelievable shade of blonde. One perfectly shaped leg was bent at the knee, and Glory could see her hand move to caress her thigh before she stretched out flat on the sand.

"Nice view, huh?"

Glory smiled. "Yes."

Wade moved closer and wrapped his arms around her shoulders. "You look better than that in a bikini."

"Love is blind, and you just proved it." Glory felt his chest move against her back as he laughed.

"I *do* mean it. Your legs are longer, and you know how I feel about long legs."

"And big boobs and compact bottoms," Glory added.

"Right." He kissed her ear. "And talent and intelligence."

Glory's smile grew, and her love for Wade seemed to consume her until her breath was coming in short gasps. His arms tightened for a moment, then he moved to stand beside her. Glory looked at his profile. A movie star's profile. Shadows played across his face, and he squinted when a ray of sunlight touched his eyes.

"What's wrong, Wade? Aren't you happy about this film?"

He sighed deeply. "I keep thinking about that old Broadway saying."

Glory tried to think of the appropriate saying, but the only one she could recall was the one about breaking a leg. "Which one?"

"You remember." He looked at her blank stare. "The stage actors say that when you're thirty-five you go to Hollywood to make pictures. You sit by the swimming pool, close your eyes for a minute, and when you open them, you're sixty."

Glory smiled. "Is that what you think will happen?" she asked gently.

He looked at the ocean again, and his voice was a whisper. "Can't you feel it, Glory? I can. I can feel my New York energy waning. I'm getting used to the star treatment. Today I found myself wondering if I'd get invited to the 'in' parties."

She felt a momentary surge of hope at his budding

disenchantment with California, but she stifled the urge to comment and rushed to reassure him. She hated to see him so worried. "We're only going to be here for three months, Wade. It takes longer than that to become a California grapefruit."

He shoved his hands into his jeans pockets and lifted his shoulders in a resigned way. "I should be happy. I've busted my rear to get here, and now I'm crying about it."

Glory let the silence talk for them for a few moments before she asked, "Were you really busting your rear to get *here?*"

He kept staring at the ocean, but Glory saw his jaw tighten until a muscle rebelled and began to jerk near his ear. "No. I wanted to be in a hit Broadway show. I've always wanted that. I always will."

"So? Why are we here?" she asked gently.

Anger deepened the color of his eyes, and Glory knew that the anger wasn't directed at her but at himself.

"Because it's so easy to be here! *I* want to earn the living, Glo! And I can't do that by pounding the pavement in New York and getting cast in shows that fold in a month." He pivoted and started to leave the room, but her hand on his arm stopped his progress.

"This earning a living thing is stupid, Wade. I can't enjoy spending money if you don't enjoy making it."

His eyes were still angry, but his voice wasn't. "I know." He tried to smile, then went to fling himself onto the couch.

Glory looked back out the glass door. The woman was gone, but the ocean was still there. The ocean and the sun were always present in California. Constant good weather bored her, and she wondered how much work she'd be able to accomplish with so much sunny weather distracting her.

"What's this?"

Glory turned to find Wade examining a plastic shopping bag filled with typed pages.

"Oh. That's Peaches' novel."

"Novel? Peaches is writing a novel?"

"Yes." Glory went to rescue the plastic bag from him. She tucked it into the closet, then relaxed in one of the recliner chairs.

"Since when has Peaches decided to write a novel?"

Glory sighed, wishing he'd drop the subject. "Since about a month ago when I told her she had a vivid imagination."

"What was it doing lying on the coffee table?"

Glory sighed again. "I'm editing it."

His eyes stretched open. "Glory . . ." It was a warning. "You're not going to—"

"I *am* going to edit it."

"I don't think that's a good idea." He rubbed the dark stubble on his chin and shook his head in a way that infuriated Glory.

"Why? You haven't even read it. What do you know?"

"Have *you* read it?"

Glory nodded.

"Well, is it any good?"

Glory forced the words past her lips. "No, it stinks."

"Precisely my point." He waved a finger at her. "If you edit that and hurt her feelings, she'll quit and we'll never find a better maid."

"Oh, rubbish!" Glory gripped the arms of the chair, digging her fingers into the soft leather. "Peaches has always wanted to write. I admire her dedication. I'm not going to slash her to ribbons! I'm going to offer constructive criticism."

A smug expression covered his face. "Constructive criticism? Like when you edited that love poem I wrote for you? *That* kind of constructive criticism?"

Glory winced at the memory. "Wade, I loved that

poem. I still have it! There were just a few minor things wrong with it—"

"I didn't write it for you to edit!" His face flushed. "Where's your sentiment? Where's your compassion?"

Glory waved her hands in surrender. "Come on! I *love* the poem, okay?"

"You marked it with a red pen! I'm surprised you didn't grade it or give it back to me for a rewrite." He glowered at her, and she shrugged.

It was hopeless to argue with him about this. He'd written that blasted poem eleven years ago, and he *still* harped about it! She breathed a sigh of relief when the telephone jangled. She leaped up from the chair and grabbed the phone in the kitchen.

"Hello?" She greeted her unknown rescuer.

"Glory Mathers?"

"Yes?" Glory sat at the kitchen table and listened to the feminine voice. She couldn't place it.

"This is Betty Harris with *Current* magazine, and I'm calling to ask if you'd consent to an interview."

"An interview?" Glory paused and looked across the room to Wade. He was reading a script, but he lowered it to meet her gaze. "With me?"

"Yes. We've been meaning to contact you for months, and we heard you're in the city now, so it's a perfect time for both of us, don't you think?"

"Well, what kind of article are we talking about?" Glory silently weighed the pros and cons. It was good timing, what with her novel slipping from second to sixth place on the best-seller list.

"Oh, just a general article about you and your writing. You know, about how you began and about your lean years. I assume there were lean years?"

Glory smiled. "Yes. Plenty of lean years." She looked at Wade and saw him nod as he dropped the script into his lap.

"We just want a profile on a successful woman. How's that sound to you?"

"Okay, I guess."

"Good! We'd like to take some photos, too. Hmmmm, when would be a convenient time for you?"

"Oh, any afternoon."

"How about next Friday at three?"

Glory glanced at the wall calendar. "That'll be fine."

"And your husband will be there?"

Glory felt the tiny hairs at the back of her neck stand on end. "Wade? No, he'll be working." She watched Wade's eyebrow descend.

"Oh, I see." Disappointment colored the woman's voice. "Well, when will he be there?"

"Why do you ask? I thought the article was to be about me." Glory stared at the wall calendar, sensing Wade's eyes upon her.

"It *is* going to be about you—and your husband. After all, your husband is part of your life."

"He has nothing to do with my career." Glory could feel Wade's frowning presence across the room.

"Well, yes, but—"

"Look." Glory took a deep breath, feeling her tongue grow sharper by the minute. "Are you planning to interview my husband through me?"

"Miss Mathers, we want to interview you, but our readers are interested in your husband, too."

"They can read about him in other magazines," Glory countered.

"Now, Miss Mathers—"

"Now, Miss Harris, just forget it." Glory fingered the telephone cord and tried to keep her voice steady. "I'm rather busy now. I'm writing a novel, so I really shouldn't take the time to sit and chat—especially about my husband."

"We'd talk mostly about your books, Miss Mathers."

"Okay." Glory twisted the cord around her fingers. "I'll consent to an interview concerning my novels and my writing. I won't answer any questions about my husband. If you want to interview him, then contact him."

"We've tried."

Glory felt her breathing stop for a few seconds as she watched her fingertips turn white where the cord was cutting into them. "I see. So you're stuck with me. Is that it?"

Wade came to stand beside her. He leaned down and mouthed, "Tell her to go to hell."

"Not quite, Miss Mathers," the voice said as Glory waved Wade away. "We *would* like to interview you, but part of your attraction is the fact that you're married to Wade Wilson. Leaving out any mention of him will make our readers feel cheated."

Glory released the cord and watched the blood color her fingertips again. "You know, Miss Harris, a few years ago your magazine interviewed me and didn't give a hoot that I was married to Wade Wilson."

The woman chuckled. "Times have changed, Miss Mathers."

Glory managed to chuckle, too. "Yes, yes, they have." She forced a pleasant note into her voice. "A few years ago, I wouldn't have passed up a chance to be interviewed by your magazine. But today I can tell you to kiss off. Good-bye, Miss Harris." Glory replaced the receiver and watched Wade collapse into one of the kitchen chairs. His laughter grated on her frayed nerves.

"I'm glad you think it's funny, Wade." She leaned back in the chair and waited for his hysterics to end.

"Who was that? *Current* magazine?"

"Yes. They've tried to reach you?"

"Yes." He wiped the tears from his eyes with his shirt sleeve. "Through the agency."

Glory stared at the telephone, wanting to rip it out of

the wall and throw it at her husband.

"Come on, Glo!" Wade touched her arm. "Why the long face? You were terrific."

Glory jerked away from his touch. "Do you know how that makes me feel? They're trying to use me! They didn't want to interview me about my work. They wanted to know if Wade Wilson is good in bed!"

"Aw, Glo." Wade pushed her hair away from her face. "Turnabout, fair play, honey."

"And what does that mean?"

"It means that I used to put up with the same crap, and now it's your turn."

Glory shook her head, confused. "I don't follow you."

Wade sighed and inched his chair closer to hers. "For years I answered that telephone and told creeps like that to kiss off. They all wanted to meet you. Nobody wanted to talk to me." His face contorted, and his mouth thinned into a bitter line. "I was Mr. Mathers. I could tell those leeches a hundred times that my name was Wilson, and they'd still call me Mathers. Free-ride Mathers."

The bitterness in his expression spilled over into his voice. Glory stared at him and wondered how she could have lived with him all these years and never seen this side of him. She'd never noticed the hurt and humiliation. She reached out to him, and her fingers wrapped around his upper arm. The muscles tensed beneath her hand.

"Why didn't you tell me how upset you were then?"

"What good would it have done?" He rolled his shoulders into a shrug. "You deserved all the recognition. You still deserve it." A wry smile twisted his mouth. "It's just that show biz outranks literature these days. Sorry, honey."

"Yes." Glory wrinkled her nose playfully. "Nobody cares whether or not *I'm* good in bed."

He bent his dark head and kissed her hand. "I care."

"I guess I'd better get used to this kind of 'fair play.'

I don't know if I'll be very good at it. I'm not much at putting on a happy face."

He tipped his head to one side and let his gaze roam over her face. "What's all this talk about not being happy? What's eating at you?"

Glory slid her hand down his arm as her gaze moved to find her children and Peaches, still involved in their sand castle. "I'm not happy. I'm not unhappy. I'm just...not..." Glory shrugged. "I don't know what I want, but I know what I *don't* want."

"Okay. Tell me what you don't want."

"I don't want to go to Hollywood parties, I don't want to move here for good, and I don't want to watch you make movies that even you can't bear to watch."

"Where on earth do you get all these ideas?" He stood to pace near her. "When have I ever made you go to Hollywood parties? If you don't want to go, don't go!" He paused and tossed her a disgusted look. "And didn't we agree that this move is temporary until further notice?"

"Arnold talks about our moving here all the time," Glory reminded him. "He'll talk you into it."

He placed his hands on the kitchen table and leaned his face toward hers. His eyes blazed with a dark fire. "You think I'm a real gutless wonder, don't you? Don't you think I have a mind of my own? *I'll* decide where I live!" He jabbed his thumb into his chest, and his voice grated with savagery.

"Okay, okay," Glory mumbled, disturbed to see him so quiveringly angry at her.

"Okay!" He straightened and went to stand by the floor-to-ceiling windows that gave them a vista of the beach and ocean. "And for your information, I'm not embarrassed to watch my movies. I'm a damn good actor."

Tears stung Glory's eyes as she stood and went to him. Something kept her from touching him, so she stood just behind him while her vision blurred with tears. "Wade, I know you're a good actor. Too good to be making these bits of fluff." She clutched his arm but received no reaction. "Wade, you used to work with the Royal Shakespeare Company!"

"Yes, and I used to make less than six thousand dollars a year."

Her fingers convulsed, wadding a bit of his sleeve into her hand. "There's more to life than a blessed buck!"

He pulled away from her, and his eyes were that scary cobalt blue that always made a shiver race up her spine. "Arnold says my face was made for the screen. I project a stronger image on the screen."

"Arnold says! Arnold says!" Glory moaned, then swallowed the wedge of emotion in her throat. "Are you in this business as just another pretty face, or because you're talented? You're a stage actor, and you won't be happy—"

"Hey!" He pointed a finger at her, and Glory saw that he was shaking. "Just because you're not happy doesn't mean I'm miserable! I'm happy, dammit!" He opened the sliding door, and Glory watched him run to the beach, passing the children and Peaches.

At the shore he stopped and started walking, setting a slow, tense pace. He walked away from the house. Away from Glory.

"You're not happy," Glory told his departing figure.

Her breath fogged the glass, and she backed away from the door. Wearily she sat at the kitchen table where bits and pieces of her novel were scattered. She wouldn't think about Wade and Hollywood now, she told herself. There was her novel to finish. Penny was waiting for it. She straightened as a cruel realization gripped her. How long had she been doing this? How long had she been retreating from the parts of her life she didn't want to confront? What good was it doing?

A tortured moan fought its way up her throat, and she pushed aside the typed pages. If only she could rewrite her life! No. It had been a good life, she amended. It just needed some editing—some "judicious" editing, as Penny would say.

She cradled her chin in her hands, wondering where to begin. Her honeymoon? No, that had been perfect. Her parents had paid for a weekend at one of New York's finest hotels as a wedding present. She and Wade had spent Friday, Saturday, and Sunday in bed, as if they were a couple of virgins who had just discovered sex.

Funny how marriage had cast a new light on their relationship, she mused. She remembered thinking that a honeymoon was silly, since she and Wade had been living together for months. But she had felt like a virgin that first night as Wade's wife. There had been a strong feeling of commitment between them, as if the vows they'd recited had seeped into their hearts and souls. That first night, when she and Wade had joined their bodies, Glory knew they were inseparable.

Ah, the ties that bind, Glory thought with a smile. There was something to be said for marriage. There was something magical in those vows said before a man of the cloth. It went far beyond promises made in the moonlight . . . far beyond desire . . . far beyond love. Wade had wanted marriage, but Glory hadn't wanted it until that first night in that hotel room. When Saturday dawned, she'd felt like a wife, and she'd liked the feeling. It was so . . . so different.

No, she wouldn't change one minute of that weekend.

Maybe . . . Yes, her character. She'd change her character during that first year of her marriage. She'd make her character more sensitive, more alert to the subtle signs. Like that time when Wade was botching all those auditions. She should have been more understanding and less wrapped up in her own career.

She recalled his expression on one particular day. He'd looked lost. He'd looked like a loser. He looked like . . .

. . . a man without an ounce of pride left.

"You didn't get the part?"

"Oh, I could've had the part." He walked past her to sit in his favorite chair by the fireplace.

"You turned it down? Wasn't the money good?" She stood beside him and wondered what she could do to erase the pain from his face.

"The money was pretty good."

"So?"

"It was a porno film."

"What? I thought it was a play!" She sat on the floor near his feet and watched his mouth dip into a deeper frown.

"So did I. But it was porn." His gaze slid over to her. "They liked me and said I could audition. All I had to do was strip."

Glory curled her upper lip in disgust. "Some audition."

"The pay was a thousand dollars a day for, oh, maybe five days. That would have come in handy."

"That kind of money we don't need." Glory folded her arms across his knees and rested her chin on her hands. "What's wrong, Wade?"

"What?" He stared at her for a moment, then shook his head. "Oh, I was just thinking." He closed his eyes, and when he opened them again, there was a bruised look in them. "I almost auditioned, Glo."

She let his words sink in. She didn't like them.

"Glory! I almost auditioned for that thing. I thought about the money and how much we needed it . . ."

"We don't need it." Glory inched closer, pressing her breasts against his shins. "We're doing okay. I just got a check in the mail, and my new agent thinks my novel has possiblities."

"Oh, Glory." He rested his head against the back of the chair and heaved a sigh. "What's wrong with me? It makes me sick to think that I'd even consider appearing in a film like that."

Glory squirmed at his feet. She felt helpless. She couldn't handle his defeat. "Wade, something will turn up for you. You've got two auditions tomorrow."

"Oh, sure. A commercial and a soap opera. Big stuff." He rolled his head from side to side. "I can't believe this! I've toured with 'class' stock companies, and I get rejected at auditions for dog food commercials." He laughed, but it was a hollow sound. "I bet those porno guys would have rejected my bod, too."

"Now, Wade. You know you've got the best bod in town—but it's mine, and I won't share it." She smiled and held her breath while she waited for his grin. It was slow in coming. "Seriously, Wade. Something will break, and you'll wonder why you worried about dog food commercials—and you'll thank your lucky stars that you didn't take that skin flick."

His smile was there now. "You're right."

"Of course I'm right!" She gathered his hands into hers. "Look, the important thing is that we've got each other." She paused and listened to her words, then laughed. "That sounds like a bad line from an old movie, doesn't it?"

"Yes." He squeezed her hands. "Trite, but true." He pulled her into his lap and framed her face with his hands. "How can you have so much confidence in me when you've never seen me act?"

She stared at him for a few moments, stunned by the truth of his words. "You're right! I haven't seen you act. You're good, though, aren't you?"

"You bet your sweet tush I'm good." One hand moved

down her body to cup her hip. "I'm too good to audition for dog food commercials and feel like a failure when I don't get them!"

She pulled his head to her breasts so that she wouldn't have to look at the pain in his face. His breath was hot against her skin, and she wanted to keep him there forever. She wanted to stroke his ego and make him feel good about himself again. She gave a mental shrug. Why not? It had always worked before.

"Wade, let's go to bed."

"To bed?" His voice was muffled against her. He lifted his head, and he was smiling. "Do you want me to audition first?"

"No." Glory placed sipping kisses on his mouth. "No audition. I've seen the merchandise, and you've got what it takes, kid."

He laughed, and this time it was real...

The memory faded, and Glory sighed, feeling the weight of her marriage settle in her heart. It was folly to attempt to find the root of her problems in her past. Wade was here to work, and it was unfair of her to burden him with her insecurities. She wasn't the type to keep quiet when something disturbed her, but maybe she should batten down the hatches until this movie was finished—if she could.

Resolve straightened her spine, and she gathered up the scattered pages of her novel. She'd try to accept the situation and make a happy little home here. She hated to see Wade upset. In his good moods, he made the world sparkle.

Glory smiled. She loved to see him happy.

6

GLORY WATCHED THE big wheels skating on their little wheels, and it was all she could do not to laugh aloud.

The tennis court lights were on, and the party guests cast long shadows as they roller-skated past her. Studio technicians, producers, directors, scriptwriters, actors, and actresses mingled along with husbands, wives, and lovers. She rested her back against the wire fence surrounding the court and wondered if these people were really having fun.

Scenes of New York friends flitted through her mind, making her long for those quiet evenings in apartments tucked in the genteel squalor of Greenwich Village and the upper West Side. Soft-spoken evenings with literary friends. Warm fireplaces, toasted marshmallows, debates about Truman and Tennessee and Lillian and Dash, gentle arguments over this new playwright and that new Shakespearean treatment, and always a midnight showing of an old movie. Tracy and Hepburn. Rock and Doris. Even Annette and Frankie.

A warmth invaded her, and sentimental tears burned her eyes. She heaved a shaky sigh. Were her dear, beloved friends gathered in some apartment in New York right now, without her? Oh, Lord! She missed them so. Didn't Wade miss them?

Wade's skates flew out from under him, and he fell with a thump on his rear. Glory couldn't keep her laughter at bay, but her laugh dwindled to a growl when Fiona Larkin helped Wade to his feet.

Glory eyed Fiona's gold lamé jogging shorts and matching tube top. Why was she dressed in a conservative, black three-piece suit when Fiona was dressed like that? She shrugged. Because she wouldn't wear what Fiona was wearing on a bet, she answered herself. Fiona linked her arm in Wade's and helped him skate to Glory. Wade rubbed his derrière and grinned.

"Now I know how a tennis ball feels."

Fiona laughed at his remark. A Sensurround laugh. She puckered her glossy lips and purred, "Poor baby."

Wade took Glory's hand. "Skate with me, Glo."

Glory started to decline but then caught Fiona's eye and changed her mind. "Okay, but remember, it's every woman for herself out there, so if you start to fall, let go of me."

Wade grinned and pulled her from the fence. They joined the others who were skating in a large circle around the court.

"Having fun?" Wade asked, dipping his head for a moment to kiss the tip of her ear.

"Not really," Glory answered honestly. "I think this is ridiculous."

"Don't be such a spoilsport." Wade gave her a disapproving frown.

"I just feel out of place, that's all."

His frown deepened. "You make yourself feel out of place, Glory. Your inferiority complex is showing."

The rubber toe of her shoe gripped the pavement, and Glory swiveled to face him. "Don't quote est to me, Wade! And don't insinuate that I feel inferior to"—she glanced around her and frowned—"these people."

Wade set his mouth in a stubborn line and pulled her to the fence. Then, hands on hips, he faced her. "What's wrong?"

"I want to go home, Wade."

"Now, Glory, let's enjoy the party. You need to get out—away from the kids."

"I'd rather be with the kids than here."

His eyes narrowed. "With me?"

The pain in his voice disarmed her, and she grasped his arm and shook her head until the words finally fell from her tongue. "No, no, Wade. That's not what I meant." She stared past him at the skaters. "It's them! I can take one or two at a time—but a whole tennis court full of them? I just can't relate to them. I don't want to, I guess." She locked her gaze with his. "I hate it here."

"Is *this* what you hate, Glo?" He waved a hand in a sweeping gesture. "Is it?"

She felt like a pricked balloon. Her being shriveled, and she collapsed against the fence. "This is all so stupid. So pointless."

Wade sighed. "If we were skating on a tennis court in New York, you'd love it. *What do you want, Glory?*" The question was forced out between straight, clenched teeth.

"I want to leave! Why don't you ever listen to me?" She wanted to fling her fists at him and make him understand how out of place she felt, but his expression told her it would be futile. They were worlds apart on this.

"No, no. What do you really want? What's bothering you?"

Glory lifted her gaze to the canopy of stars. "I wish we could be like we were in New York right after we married."

"You mean poor?"

"No. Happy."

She listened to him breathe for a few seconds before he whispered, "In other words, you're not happy now."

"Are you?" Her gaze left the stars to find the sparkles

in his eyes. "Are you happy, Wade? Sometimes I feel as if we've drifted apart, and we're too lazy to reach out to one another."

"Wade! Come join the party!"

Glory looked past him to find the shimmering figure of Fiona. The tube top was taut, and Glory could see the swell of Fiona's nipples as she whizzed past. Fiona belonged here.

"Wade?"

"Yes?"

"Do you have any love scenes with Fiona?"

"Yes."

"Bed scenes?"

"Yes." He touched her arm, running his hand from her shoulder to her wrist. "Are you jealous? Is that it?"

"Should I be?"

Wade rested one hand against the fence behind her, and Glory watched his white pullover move with his breathing. "Okay, Glo. Now let's go back to the party before people start talking."

She hated him for not easing her mind. "You still care about what people think and say about you, don't you?"

He closed his eyes for a moment, and when his lashes lifted, Glory could see irritation shadow his eyes. "Please, Glory. Please?"

"You go ahead. I've got to go inside for a minute." Glory rolled away from him and skated to the swinging gate. She pushed through the gate and stomped across the grounds, not bothering to remove the skates. They felt like lead weights on her feet, and her knees were weak by the time she reached the patio doors. Her skate wheels left bits of grass and dirt on the tiled floors as she wheeled toward the bathroom.

Glory closed the bathroom door and sat before the vanity in the plush anteroom. She examined herself in the oval mirror. She looked pale and shaken. Why did

Wade insist on pleasing those morons? He wasn't enjoying himself; he was just here to play their stupid games. She balled her hands into fists and pounded the marble table. Grow up, Wade! Grow up. Who cares what they think, what they say about you behind your back?

Someone knocked on the bathroom door, and Glory cleared her throat and fixed a tranquil expression on her face.

"Yes, come in!"

The bathroom door swung open, and Fiona entered and stood behind Glory, examining her reflection.

"Are you okay? You seemed upset, so I thought I'd check on you."

Glory wanted to scream in frustration, but she forced the hysterical notion from her mind. "Yes, I'm ... fixing my makeup." She rummaged through her purse.

"Oh, okay. Don't be too long. You're missing all the fun." Fiona flashed Glory her fabulous smile. "Love your suit."

Fiona's reflection left the room, and Glory tossed her purse onto the table. Was she jealous of Fiona? She tipped her head to one side and examined her large green eyes and thick brown hair.

"Say it isn't so, Glory," she begged herself, but her reflection refused to answer. Glory cradled her head in her hands and held her breath to kill the sob in her constricted throat.

She needed to go back to the tennis court. Wade wanted her there. If she stayed here much longer, people would begin to think—

Glory curled her fingers around a smooth object and flung it across the room. She watched her compact mirror shatter and splinter against the wall.

Pieces of glass glinted on the carpet. The carpet? The tile. Yes. Pieces of glass glinted on the tile ...

* * *

...and she stared at them and felt her composure break into similar fragments.

"Wade, you're making me nervous."

"Okay. Okay." His voice was consoling. "I'll clean up the glass." He dried his hands on a towel and fetched the broom and dustpan from the closet. "It's just a broken cup. Nothing to cry about."

"I'm not crying about the cup, and you know it!" She sat in one of the kitchen chairs and watched her hands tremble. "Why can't we just continue with the present relationship? Why complicate everything?"

"I don't see marriage as a complication." Slivers of glass tinkled against the metal dustpan. "I love you."

"I know." She wiped the tears from her face. "Let's just hold off for a while."

"Glory, my parents are coming to visit in two weeks." He straightened and dumped the glass into the garbage can. "I don't want to hide my relationship with you."

"Hide? Why do we have to hide?" Her fingers swiped at her face and came away wet. "Just tell them we live together."

"Glory, my dad is a minister! My mother is a saint! They won't understand. They'll be hurt."

A hysterical giggle gurgled in her throat. "I don't believe you, Wade. You're a grown man! Surely your parents have recognized that fact."

His shoulders slumped and he pulled the stopper from the sink drain to let the sudsy water escape. "I love them, Glo. I love you." He left the sink and sat in the chair opposite her. His fingers took hers. "Please, marry me. It will make things so much easier for both of us."

"My mother knows we live together, and she hasn't disowned me or committed suicide."

"Your mother is weird." He tightened his grip on her fingers. "I love her, but she *is* different. And your dad— well, nothing ever bothers him."

Glory sighed. "I don't think I'm ready for marriage, Wade. I'm so selfish. I wouldn't make a good wife. You'd be miserable."

He smiled. "Things wouldn't change that much, Glo. Look, we get along now, don't we?"

"Y—e—s," Glory agreed as she studied his fingers. Long, sensitive fingers that curled around hers for a perfect fit. "But you'd make demands on me, and then I'd blow up and kick you out."

"I won't make unreasonable demands on you. I promise."

"I don't know." She examined his fingers again and searched for another excuse.

Wade intercepted her. "We'll have a fifty-fifty relationship. We'll share everything, and I won't interfere with your writing."

"Oh, no?" She shook her head. "Wade, there's no such thing as a fifty-fifty relationship. It's always sixty-forty."

"I'll take the sixty part." He wiggled his eyebrows comically.

Glory laughed and felt herself slipping into his reasoning. She was drowning. Going under for the third time. She managed one last effort. "Let's think about it a while longer."

"We can't. My parents . . . what will they think?"

She yanked her hands from his. "This has nothing to do with your straitlaced parents! I won't marry you just to please your parents. Forget it!" She stood and walked from the room. Wade was right behind her.

"Glory, if you don't marry me, I'll leave. I will! I'm not kidding."

She turned in the threshold of her study. "You can't come in here, Wade. This is *my* study. Remember?" She saw his face flush darkly before she slammed the door.

Glory stumbled to the couch and draped herself over

the cushions. Her eyes focused on the stack of papers on her desk. Magazine articles. Book reviews. Things that editors were waiting for. Her gaze moved to the hill of typed pages on the windowsill. Her novel. Her pet project that no one was waiting for.

The door swung open, and Wade faced her. His eyes were that midnight blue that meant he was on the verge of no return.

"It's not just that I want to please my parents. I want to please you—always." He made a gesture of pure frustration. "I don't want anyone else to have you. I'm selfish, too, and I know when I've got a good thing."

"You've already got me, Wade." She eased herself to a sitting position. "Marriage won't change that."

"Right."

He sat next to her, curving his hands around her neck. For a crazy moment, Glory thought he was going to strangle her, but his hands were as gentle as his voice.

"So why fight it? I'm old-fashioned. I want you to marry me."

Submerged for the third time, Glory smiled. "I'm keeping my maiden name."

The expression on his face was the closest thing to rapture she'd ever seen.

His lips found hers, whispering across them. "Keep your name, Glo. Just take me..."

Glory stood and gathered the pieces of her shattered compact, a smile resting on her lips as the memory nestled firmly into the corners of her mind. She looked up when someone knocked at the door, but before she could respond, Wade stepped into the room.

"What happened?"

Glory sighed. "I threw it."

"Why?"

She shrugged and dumped the remains into a mink-lined trash receptacle. She stared at the furry trash can and wondered what sort of person would actually buy something like that.

"If you'll take off those skates, I'll take you home."

She looked down at the ridiculous roller skates and sat on the vanity bench to remove them. "Gladly. Did I spoil the party for you?"

"Sort of, but don't worry about it. I'm ready to leave."

She handed him the skates, then let her gaze devour him. How could she pick a fight with him? He was so cute. She grinned, letting her eyes travel the length of his dark trousers and white pullover.

"What's so funny?"

"I was just thinking about your proposal of marriage. Do you remember that?"

"Sure. Are you regretting your answer?" He held out a hand to her, and she took it.

"No. Are you?"

His fingers wrapped around her hand, and his eyes suddenly shone with passion. "Let's go home, Glo. I want to get something straight between us."

His mouth teased her breast, and Glory twined her fingers in the thickness of his hair. The peace that had been eluding her during the past weeks slowly consumed her as Wade continued to worship her body.

Slowly he rolled onto his back, taking her with him, and Glory smoothed the hair on his chest with her palms. When her hands brushed over the nubs of flesh nestled there, Wade moaned and his hands cupped her hips. Planting tiny kisses upon his chest, Glory inched lower until her mouth found his muscled stomach. She touched the tip of her tongue to his moist skin and traced the path of a rib. Would she ever grow tired of touching him? she wondered as his fingers combed through her hair to create a fan of it across his chest. Her hands found him, and she marveled at the pulsating strength she held.

Her name burst from him as he shifted to rest his body atop hers again. In the glow of the light cast by the perfumed candles near the bed, Glory watched him watching her as he slowly came to her. She sucked in her breath, always surprised at the glorious burning sensation she felt when they joined. It was miraculous to be surprised by a man you'd made love to countless times.

The niggling problems that had built up over the past few years dissipated as Wade increased his tempo and Glory sought to match it. His mouth found hers, and his tongue created a delicious friction as he explored with infinite assurance. She sensed the approach of his final burst of passion, and she held him close, kneading the flexing muscles in his shoulders. Pressure grew within her until she was a thrashing blur of desire. His name filled her mouth just as he stilled, then quivered violently.

The musky fragrance of their lovemaking wafted to her, and Glory stroked his hair, her fingertips finding the damp tendrils at his temples. Her fingers glided over his cheekbones, and her thumbs caressed the dimple in his chin.

Dusky lashes lifted to reveal dark blue eyes, and the corners of his mouth twitched into a smile. Glory returned his smile, and an understanding as old as love itself passed between them.

"I'm sorry about tonight, Wade." The statement escaped her before she had time to analyze it.

"I'm not." The tip of his tongue slid down the bridge of her nose. "I think this little party has been a great success."

She smoothed the hair from his forehead. "I agree. I was referring to the other party."

He rolled to one side and propped his head in one hand. "It's going to take some adjustment, Glory. I understand that."

"I've been checking on the school system here, Wade. I really don't like the idea of the kids going to school here. Adam loves his school in New York."

Wade closed his eyes for an instant and sighed. "We don't have to think about that now. The film will be wrapped before school starts."

"And what about the next film? Wade, it's not just the two of us anymore. We have the children to think about."

"Don't you think I know that? They're my kids, too." He fell sideways onto his back and stared at the ceiling. "The kids aren't suffering. They love the beach."

Glory could feel him pulling away from her. Why did she have to talk about this now? It had been so good just a few minutes ago. She rolled over, resting her cheek against his chest. Automatically his hand came to caress her waist. Glory listened to the distant sound of the ocean and found herself missing the scream of sirens and the blare of horns.

"I've been talking to Arnold."

The mere mention of Arnold's name drenched her with sticky gloom. She waited, knowing there was more.

"He's dealing with Jason Bernard about his next film. Bernard is interested in casting me as the lead."

"Bernard usually shoots on location. Where is it?" Glory held her breath.

"They're talking about Yugoslavia."

"Oh, great!" She heard the acidic irony in her voice, and she lifted her head in time to see Wade frown. "Wade, Arnold is so entrenched here that I don't think he ever knows who's casting what on Broadway. He never even mentions plays or anything like that."

"So?"

Glory inched upward until she was eye-to-eye with Wade. "So why don't you talk to him about that? Why don't you tell Arnold to scout Broadway for a change?"

"Glo, did it ever occur to you that I might not want to be in a play right now? Did you ever consider the fact that I might enjoy making films?"

"You don't." Glory battled with his gaze, challenging him to contradict her.

"I do."

It was like a death blow. Glory shut her eyes and pulled her bottom lip between her teeth as the import of those two words took its toll. Her voice was weak. "But, what about your dream to act on stage, Wade?"

"Broadway will still be there a few years from now." His hand smoothed through her hair. "Honey, do you remember how thrilled you were when magazines started calling you about doing articles for them?"

She nodded, unable to push words past her lips.

"I remember. And I remember thinking that some-day—someday I'd know that same feeling. That day is here, Glo. Producers and directors are asking for *me*. I'm working, and I love it. Understand?"

Again she could only nod.

"With every film I gain more confidence in myself. When I go to Broadway, I want to go there with clout. My days of begging are over, Glo."

"What about me?"

His eyes widened. "What about you?"

"*My* career, Wade. My publisher and my agent are in New York."

A mildly chastising expression blanketed his face. "Glo, you can write anywhere."

"Yugoslavia?"

He smiled and shook his head. "Nothing's firm on that. You know I wouldn't commit myself to anything without discussing it with you first."

"And my opinion will count for something?"

"It always has."

She lay on her back while her mind wrestled with

itself. If her opinion counted, what was she doing here? She wanted to voice the question, but she wasn't ready for his reaction. The word "selfish" reared its head again, and she closed her eyes to it. She wasn't being fair. They had discussed this move, and they'd struck a compromise. Was she angry because everything wasn't falling into neat patterns that benefitted her?

His leg pressed against hers, and the crisp hair that covered his skin rasped across her smooth thigh. She turned her head, and his lips covered hers. A warm, searching hand quested beneath the sheet until it found the rounded softness of her breast. He lifted his mouth from hers.

"I have a bed scene with Fiona tomorrow morning, Glo. I need to get some practice in."

Glory felt her mouth drop open before she saw the twinkle in his eyes. She slapped him on the shoulder and laughed with him.

"You have your nerve, Wade Wilson!"

His lips brushed over hers. "I have you, Glory, and that's all I've ever wanted."

Glory smiled. She loved his way with words.

7

GLORY REACHED INTO the grocery sack and withdrew the magazine, then tossed the sack into the back seat for the children to fight over.

"The Archie comic book is mine!"

Adam's voice boomed in the car, and Glory turned around and glared at him.

"Quiet, please. Damon, give Dani the Batman comic book. I bought the Superman comic for you." She turned back to stare at Wade's photo on the cover of the movie magazine. The headline above his picture sent a blaze of anger coursing through her. *Wade Wilson: Hollywood's newest sex symbol says he likes his women soft and pliant.* Disgust wormed within her as she flipped through the magazine to find the companion article.

"That's Daddy!" Dani reached over the seat to point at Wade's picture. "What's it say about him, Mommy?"

"Read your comic book, Dani." Glory folded the magazine and ran her eye over the photo. It was a publicity shot taken during the making of his last film.

"Are we going to the studio?" Damon asked.

"In a minute." Glory focused on the text and felt her fury increase.

Sitting in his trailer on the set of *Twisting Turns*, Wade is a wonderful blend of mischievous boy and sensuous man. He smiles, and his voice is resonant as he discusses his favorite subject—women.

"I like women who are soft and pliant. That type of woman brings out the best in a man. Aggressive women bring out the worst in a man. I don't like to compete with women. I like to appreciate them, and I can't when they're into that I-can-do-anything-better-than-you trip."

Glory closed the magazine and felt her blood boil. If he'd said that, she'd kill him! She switched on the Mercedes' engine and backed from the parking space. Aiming the nose of the sleek automobile toward the studio, she forced herself to calm down. Chances were he hadn't said that, she reasoned. It didn't sound like him. Did it?

At the movie lot, she was directed to the *Twisting Turns* sound stage, and the children began jumping up and down in the back seat as they pointed out movie stars.

"That's John Wayne!" Adam grabbed her shoulder as she parked the car.

Glory looked at the man who was dressed in a cowboy outfit. "No it's not."

"It is, too!"

"Adam, dear, John Wayne is dead."

"Huh?" Adam blinked. "I watched him on television yesterday."

Glory turned in the seat to meet Adam's green eyes, eyes the same color as her own. Adam looked confused, then his expression cleared, and he blushed.

"Oh, yeah." He shrugged, gave her that halfhearted grin he was so adept at, and opened the car door.

Glory walked behind the children and watched them attack the guard at the door to the soundstage. The guard pinned her with a steely blue glare.

"Hello!" Glory tried to sound cheerful. "I'm Glory

Mathers, Wade Wilson's wife. Can we go into the studio?"

"Nope." The guard placed his hands on his hips.

Glory issued a short laugh. "Well, can you tell Wade we're out here?"

"Nope."

"Why not?" She tried to keep the smile from slipping from her lips.

The guard swung his head in the direction of a red light above the door. "They're filming."

Glory stared at the light and smiled when it turned green. "Not anymore." She pointed to the green light. "Now can we go in?"

"Nope. I'll have to see some identification."

Glory drew a calming breath. "Okay, okay." She rummaged through her purse, and her hand found the small cylinder of Mace inside. She smiled as her fingers closed around it. I'll give him some identification! No, no, a calmer voice inserted. She was being aggressive instead of pliant and soft. She pulled out her wallet and flipped through it to find her driver's license. The door to the soundstage swung open, and Arnold emerged.

"Arnold!" She dropped the wallet back into her purse. "Can you identify me to this man, please?"

Arnold looked at her. He looked at the guard. He looked at her again. "Why?"

Fiery rage burned through her. "Arnold! I'm trying to get into the studio to see Wade. Tell this man who I am!"

Arnold flinched. "It's okay. She's Wade's wife." He puffed out his chest. "Besides, we're finished in there for the day. Let her in, Jim."

Jim gave Glory the once-over, then stepped aside. "Go on."

"Thanks ever so much!" Glory stalked onto the soundstage, the children following behind her. She squinted into the darkness, then headed for the oasis of bright light. The children started to run past her, but she put out an arm to block them.

"Don't give me any trouble. Just behave."

They nodded and kept two paces behind her as she moved toward the action. Stepping carefully over cables, Glory edged around lights and cameras. Fiona Larkin's perfectly pitched laugh chimed as Glory approached the set. Fiona and Wade were standing in what was supposed to be a motel room, and another woman stood beside Wade.

Fiona spotted Glory, and she fluttered her eyelashes. "Look who's here!"

Wade turned and arched one brow. "Glo! What's up?"

"Nothing. I came here to talk you into taking us to dinner."

"Oh." He glanced at the women. "Excuse me?" He scooped Dani into his arms. "Let's go to my trailer, and I'll change."

"Sounds great." Glory forced a smile to her lips as she nodded toward the women. "Nice to see you."

Wade stalked toward a white trailer that had his name printed on the door. The children rushed past him to fight for possession of a love seat. Glory perched in a director's chair and watched as Wade began unbuttoning his shirt.

"I'm beat. You really want to go out and eat?"

"Yes."

"But I've been working all day and—"

"So have I." Glory fixed a firm expression on her face.

"Yes, I know." He sighed and stripped the shirt from his body. "How about if we pick up some fried chicken and—"

"Yeah!" the children chorused.

Glory gave them a murderous stare before turning back to Wade. He was stepping out of his trousers, and she watched the long muscles in his thighs flex. "Wade, is that your idea of going out to dinner?"

"I just don't want to get all dressed up, Glo. I'm bushed." He tossed his clothes onto a daybed and rummaged through a closet for a pair of jeans and a work shirt.

"We can go to a casual restaurant."

"McDonald's!" Adam shouted.

"Not *that* casual," Glory interjected.

"What have you got there?" Wade sat on the floor next to her and tapped the magazine she held.

"Oh. It's got an article about you in it. Take a look at that headline, Wade." She held it out for him, noticing his frowning face as he took it from her.

"Glory, when did you start reading trash like this?" He turned to the article and scanned it.

"I couldn't resist that one. The headline caught my attention."

He glanced up at her, read her expression, then tossed the issue across the room. Adam laughed, and Damon left the love seat to retrieve the magazine.

"I hope you're not going to ask me to discuss that drivel." He ran a hand through his hair, mussing it slightly.

Glory sighed, suddenly aware of the signs of fatigue he was emitting. She smoothed his hair back into place. "I'm sorry, Wade. I don't know why I'm being so ornery."

"Well, when you find out, will you tell me? I'd like to know why you're so eager to pick fights these days."

"Are we going to eat or what?" Adam crossed his arms and glowered at them.

"We're going to eat, tough guy." Wade pushed himself to his feet and gestured toward the door. "Last one to the car is a lead Frisbee."

The children giggled and dashed to the door. Glory eased herself from the chair, feeling guilty for having been so testy with Wade. It had been one of those days when nothing seemed to go right.

Once they were ensconced in the Mercedes, Glory spotted Wade's silver Ferrari. "What about your car, Wade?"

"I'll have the studio send a limo for me in the morning." He winked at her. "I'm a star, you know."

"Yes, I know."

"Is The Grotto all right?"

She stared at him for a moment. "The Grotto?"

"Sure." He turned onto the boulevard, and palm trees shadowed the car. "How does that sound?"

The kids moaned and sighed and fumed. Glory smiled and felt loved and pampered.

"Yes. The Grotto's fine. I like their food."

"Okay." He glanced in the rearview mirror. "Put a lid on it, kids. They have chicken and hamburgers there, too." He stopped at a street light and his eyes found Glory's. "You shouldn't believe everything you read, Glo. Remember when those magazine gossips predicted that we'd be divorced within a couple of years?"

"Yes. They said it wouldn't last." Glory frowned, recalling how hurt she'd been when she'd read those articles.

"Right. They said that an out-of-work actor wasn't a good match for a successful author." He laughed softly. "And here we are, ten years later."

"There've been a few changes. You're working now."

"Yes, thank heavens." He sighed, then accelerated through the intersection. "I know what you'll order."

"What?"

"Cabbage rolls. Right?"

"Ummmm. That sounds delicious." She looked at her wedding ring. "Thanks, Wade."

He shrugged. "S'okay, partner."

Glory could already taste the cabbage rolls, and her

mouth began to water. Cabbage rolls. Like the ones they made at Sister Wind's in New York. Juicy and spicy and exotic. She could see them in her mind, steaming on her plate. She started to cut one; then watched it roll . . .

. . . into her lap.

"Oh, crap!" She bit her tongue and glanced around the table at Wade, his father, and his mother.

"Did it stain your dress?" Mrs. Wilson, the saint, looked at the orange grease spot on Glory's white maternity dress.

So much for purity, Glory thought. "Yes. It's stained."

"Wait a moment." Saint Wilson produced a vial from her purse, opened it, and dabbed several drops of clear liquid onto the stain. She rubbed the liquid into the fabric with her napkin. "It's stain remover," she explained, still rubbing.

This woman carries stain remover in her handbag? Glory was amazed, stunned, and irrationally disgusted. What else did she have in that handbag? Insect repellent? A first-aid kit? A miniature sewing machine?

"There!" Saint Wilson inspected her work. "When it's washed, you won't be able to tell."

"That's wonderful," Glory mumbled, still in shock. "Thank you, Mrs. Wilson."

"That's quite all right, dear. I know that dress cost a pretty penny, and I know you two are on a . . ." She paused to purse her lips. "Tight budget."

"How much are they going to pay you for that panty hose commercial, son?" the minister asked.

Wade fidgeted. He didn't like to quote salaries. "Enough to get us out of the hole for a while, Dad."

"Sure, we're doing fine!" Glory offered. "Remember, I sold my novel."

The minister nodded. Wade smiled. The saint patted Glory's hand.

"It's so nice that you can write," the saint said. "Of course, once that little bundle comes, you won't have time for writing."

"I *will* write," Glory objected. "The baby won't keep me from that."

"You'll see, my dear. I raised one, and *I* know."

"You're not a writer."

"Glory thinks writers are a species unto themselves," Wade said with an indulgent tone to his voice.

Glory glared at him. "That's because we are—just like actors. Will the baby keep you from *your* career?"

Wade shook his head. "No. The only thing that keeps me from my career is the stupidity of casting directors."

The truth pierced Glory's indignant armor, and she was at a loss for words. It must have affected the minister and the saint, too, because table talk centered on the good and bad aspects of the food and service for the rest of the evening. Other subjects were taboo.

Wade and Glory finally dropped his parents off at the hotel, then made their way to their apartment. Glory followed Wade into the bedroom and watched him strip off his clothes.

"Do you think they enjoyed the evening?"

"I guess so," he answered, dropping his clothes onto the floor.

"Hang up your clothes. Did *you* enjoy the evening?"

"Not really." He started hanging up his clothes, and his movements were rebellious. "I get tired of making excuses to Mom and Dad about why I'm not making a living. It's worse now that the baby is due any day."

She felt helpless and responsible. "You should be happy."

He carried his clothes to the closet and stuffed them inside. "All I can think of are hospital and doctor bills."

"Well, stop thinking about them. I've got an advance on the novel, and the rest will be here soon. We can pay the bills."

"You can pay the bills." He flung himself onto the bed and pulled the sheet up to his chin in a gesture that infuriated Glory.

"It's *our* money!" Glory sighed. She was tired of this argument. "Let's be happy, Wade. Please?"

He sighed. "Okay."

Glory sighed. "You sound so convincing." She began undressing but kept one eye on him. He was staring at the ceiling, and he never blinked. She slipped into her nightgown and thought what a wonderful circus tent it would make. Slipping in beside him, Glory touched her leg to his. He inched away.

"I know I had to talk you into this parenting thing, Wade. But you wait and see; you'll be so proud of us when you see our baby. Don't be unhappy. Or if you really have to, be unhappy, but try to *act* happy, at least."

He still didn't blink, but he rolled his eyes to the side to see her. "Do you have any idea how much it costs to raise a child?"

Glory slammed her fist into the pillow beside his head. He blinked. "Do you know how irritating you are? I'll tell you! If Trudy walked through that door right now, I'd say, 'Take him! He's all yours. He's a whiner who values life by how much money he's making!'" Glory swallowed a sob and struggled out of bed. She felt like a paperweight. A huge paperweight trying to keep her marriage from flying about in a crazy funnel where there was nothing to hang on to.

"No you wouldn't."

"I wouldn't what?" She sat at the dresser and brushed her hair with angry, swift strokes.

"You wouldn't tell Trudy that. You're crazy about me."

Glory moved her gaze to find his reflection in the mirror. His rakish smile dissipated her anger, and she felt an answering smile curve her mouth.

"Come back here, beautiful."

"Are you talking to me?" She dropped the brush and placed her hands upon her protruding midsection. *"This is beautiful?"*

"And how." The last was a lazy growl. He propped himself up on his elbows and crooked a finger at her. "All of that is mine, and I want to hold it."

She rose slowly, carefully, loving him for making her feel beautiful and needed. She started toward him, but the swift, sharp pain in her back stopped her. She sucked in her breath and waited. The baby kicked once, twice, then all was quiet on the labor front.

A wave of wonder washed over her as she stood there, her vision blurred by that stab of pain. Wonder. Total, sweet wonder such as she'd never known before. Not even when her doctor had told her she was pregnant and she'd had nothing to show for it but a half-empty bottle of Pepto-Bismol had she felt this flowering glow. She smiled, feeling like a walking, breathing miracle.

"Glo? Glory?"

Wade's face edged its way into her watery vision. She examined the deep lines between his eyes.

"Glory, what's wrong?"

She liked the worry in his voice. He was an outsider. She and the baby were the only ones 'in' on this one. Suddenly she felt sorry for Wade.

"Come back to bed with me, Wade. Let's count contractions."

"Oh, my God! You're kidding! Tell me you're kidding!"

Glory shook her head and placed her fingertips against his cool lips. "Don't. Not now. Come on." She grasped his hand and pulled him to the bed. "Let's rest. We'll need it."

"I'm going to call Mom and Dad." He sat on the bed and reached for the extension telephone. "They'll know what to do about this."

Glory placed her hand on his shoulder and settled herself beside him. "I'm sure your mother has an obstetrician in her purse, but *I* know what to do. This might just be a false alarm. We'll wait and see. Now help me lie down."

Gently he helped her to lie flat, then he slid his body beside hers and propped his head in one hand. He stared at her in a probing, soul-shaking examination. Then he nodded, and one corner of his mouth lifted. "Okay. We'll wait."

The rhythm of the New York traffic drifted into the bedroom, and Glory closed her eyes. She could visualize the red, yellow, and green lights. She could see the taxis and the pedestrians. She could see the skyscrapers and the rows of apartment buildings. She could see the city she loved. The city where she would raise her red-faced, brawling, squalling child. He or she would be a survivor of this tough/tender city. An achiever.

Pain. This time black and ominous and telling. The tip of it found her back again and drove in slowly, taking her breath and squeezing tears from her eyes. She cried out and clutched something. Wade's arm. A death-lock. His voice was far away and near. It trembled and quaked and added to her misery. Air filled her lungs again in quick, short gasps. The sound was familiar. Didn't she do this when she and Wade made love? How curious. How ironic. How wonderful.

Glory opened her eyes, and Wade's face was thrust close to hers. Beads of perspiration glistened on his forehead and upper lip. Her eyes were bright with moisture.

"Wade." Glory's voice cracked. "Wade, don't. It's okay. I'm okay."

He buried his face against the side of her neck. "Oh, Glory. I love you." He shook his head and took a deep, shuddering breath. "I want the baby. I'm just scared.

I'm scared that I'll fail."

She gathered his hair into her hands and rocked back and forth. "Wade, you're not a failure. You've never failed me, and you won't fail at being a father either. Now hush. Let's just hold each other."

He nodded and lifted his head. He kissed the tip of her nose. "Does it hurt real bad?"

She smiled, thinking he sounded like a little boy. "Yes, but I'll make it. The baby is the one who's in for a rough time."

"You're sure you're okay? You cried out a minute ago."

"Get used to it, partner."

His eyebrows descended. "Should I count contractions?"

Glory squeezed his arm. "Yes. You time me, okay?"

He nodded and reached for his wristwatch. "I'm ready."

"So am I."

She knew that she wasn't, but she didn't want to frighten him. She looked at him and wondered if the child she carried would look like him. Would her baby have those trusting blue eyes? Would her baby have that touseled black hair?

Glory tried to relax, waiting for this chapter in their lives to end. This was very much like writing, she thought, except that someone else held the pen, and she and Wade were the characters—just waiting to see what came next. It was interesting being a character, for a change...

Now Glory blinked away the sweet memories and looked across the table at her husband. He oozed self-confidence, and she was struck by how much he'd changed since that night so many years ago. The set of his shoulders was straight, and a maturity was stamped on his features that hadn't been there eight years ago. That had been the first and only time she'd seen Wade close to tears. When the twins had been born, he'd handled the situation like a pro.

"How'd you like the cabbage rolls?"

She looked down at her empty plate. "Pretty well, I guess."

"When I grow up, I'm going to be a waiter."

Glory looked at Adam, surprised at his announcement. "A waiter?"

"Yeah. You were a waiter once, weren't you, Daddy?"

A tiny smile flickered over Wade's face. "Yes, but not by choice. I thought you wanted to be an astronaut."

"I did, but I've changed my mind."

"It's so dark in here I can't even see my hamburger!" Damon poked at the remains of his burger and frowned.

"You don't have to see it, kid. Just eat it." Wade ruffled Damon's dark hair. "Slowpoke."

"This is called intimate lighting, Damon." Glory glanced around the secluded alcove.

"We're sitting here because it's so dark people can't see Daddy." Adam fixed an expression of pride on his face. "Isn't that right?"

Wade shrugged. "That's right, kiddo." Wade heaved a dramatic sigh. "Ah, the price of fame."

Glory examined his contented expression. "You're happy, aren't you?"

The look of contentment changed into a scowl. "Are we back to that again?"

She shook her head. "No. But you *are* happy, aren't you?"

He nodded as he selected a fry from Dani's plate and grinned when she slapped his hand. "I feel good about this film so far. Tim Simpson is a fine director." He stole another fry and popped it into his mouth. "How's your novel coming, Glo?"

She shrugged. "Slow."

"What's the problem?"

"I miss New York."

She jumped slightly when he muttered an oath under his breath, then sent him a warning glance.

"I'm sorry, but we've only been here for a month! If you're trying to make me feel guilty, you're succeeding."

"I'm not trying to make you feel anything. You asked a question, and I answered it." Glory inched back her chair: "Are you ready to go?"

"Yes!"

She waited at the restaurant entrance for him to pay their bill. The cashier was all thumbs as she took Wade's credit card. Poor thing, Glory thought. She's blinded by Wade's star quality.

The ride home was punctuated only by the children's voices, and Glory found herself wishing she hadn't answered Wade so honestly. Sometimes a wife had to lie.

The beach house loomed ahead of them, all glass and weathered beams. She thought of the first home they'd shared—that two-bedroom apartment with its second-hand furnishings. She remembered how she'd longed for something . . . something just like this beach house.

Once inside, the children headed for their bedrooms to play video games. Wade settled himself on the four-cushioned couch and flipped on the television set. Glory picked up the remote-control device and erased the picture from the screen. Slowly Wade turned his head until his eyes found her where she was standing in the center of the huge living room.

"Something on your mind?"

"Do you wish we hadn't had children?"

His blue eyes rolled heavenward. "No, I don't. Is that why you turned off the set? To ask me *that?*"

She went to him, perching on the edge of the couch. He shifted, giving her more room. "I was thinking about when I went into labor with Adam. You were full of doubts then. Remember?"

"Yes, but that was years ago." He glanced down, watching her fingers unbutton his shirt. "Would you like to go back to New York and visit?"

Her fingers stilled. "With or without you?"

"Without. I can't leave now."

She pulled the shirt from his waistband. "I'll pass."

"Glory, I'm doing everything I can to make you happy. You miss New York, so why don't you go back for a few days?"

"Because I'd miss you more." She pressed her palms against his warm skin. "Wouldn't you miss me?"

"Yes. Yes, I would." His hands pushed through the hair at her temples. "Come on, give. What's troubling you?"

She sighed, amazed at how well he knew her. "I don't want you to go to Yugoslavia, Wade."

He grinned. "I'm not crazy about the idea myself. I haven't been offered the part yet, Glory."

"But what if you are?"

"Then I'll think about it." He tipped her head forward, and his lips brushed across her cheek. "We'll both think about it long and hard."

"I read in *Variety* today that Bob Farleigh is getting ready to cast his new stage drama."

"Is that so?" Mild amusement stirred in his eyes.

"Yes." Glory smiled. "You respect his work, don't you?"

"Yes. The question is, does he respect mine?"

"That's the question." Glory curled her hands against his chest. "Am I being too pushy?"

"Do you have to ask?"

Glory sighed wearily. "If I'm sticking my nose where it doesn't belong, just tell me."

"Come here, you." He pulled her toward him until she was lying at his side, pressed close to his body. "I'll ask Arnold to look into it, but if the feedback from New York is lukewarm, that's it. Understand?"

"Yes."

"You know, you'd probably get more work done on your novel if you'd stop reading *Variety.*"

"You sound like Penny."

"Well, for once I agree with Penny." He rubbed his cheek against the top of her head. "Glory, you're pushing. You married an actor, and an actor doesn't work in one place all the time."

"We've been in New York ten years," she reminded him.

"I wasn't working much during those first few years. You were making the living."

The bitterness in his voice lifted her head, and she looked at him. "You really resented that, didn't you?"

"With every fibre of my being."

The grave sincerity in his eyes startled her. "You're a good actor, Wade. I never suspected how much it upset you."

His hands smoothed down her back, the warmth of him penetrating her silk blouse. "I hope, from now on we'll continue to be faced with career decisions. I won't always be able to please you with those decisions, Glory. I know we have the kids to think about, but we have ourselves and our work to think about, too."

"I know." She lifted her face for his kiss, willing him to stop talking. She didn't want to face their future now, not when his hands were tracing circles on her back and his mouth was hungry against her own. In the distance, she could hear Peaches getting the kids ready for bed. She'd have to go in soon and say good night to them. But not now.

Wade pulled his mouth from hers, and his eyes told

her all she needed to know. "I've got an early call in the morning. Let's go to bed."

She rose from the couch with him and wrapped her arms around his waist as they strolled toward the staircase that led to the second level and their privacy.

In their bedroom, Wade began to undress her slowly, pausing every so often to place sipping kisses upon her face, her breasts, her stomach.

Glory smiled. She loved the way he loved her.

 **8**

EDNA MATHERS'S KITCHEN had changed little in the twenty-five years she'd reigned over it. Sitting at the Formica-topped kitchen table, Glory eyed the built-in dishwasher and the microwave oven, which were the only additions made since Edna and Howard had moved in. Glory sipped her coffee and recalled a time when she'd watched her mother and her mother's friends sit at this table drinking coffee and trading gossip. She'd longed for the day when she could join the women's circle. Well, she was finally a member, she thought with a sigh, and it wasn't nearly as exciting as she'd imagined.

"I'm surprised you'd leave Wade alone in California," Edna said as she pulled a sheet of macaroons from the oven. "But I'm glad you came back home. I miss you when you're away."

"Wade isn't alone," Glory said. "I left Peaches with him."

"Oh, Lord!" Edna clucked her tongue. "That's worse than being alone. Poor Wade." She turned off the oven and glanced at her daughter. "I know you like Peaches, dear, but I swear she has bats in her belfry."

"Mother, she'd have to be a little nuts to work for us. We aren't exactly Ozzie and Harriet, you know."

Edna set a platter in front of Glory. "Macaroons! Your favorite." She beamed a mother's smile as she took one of the chairs at the table. "You'll be here at least a week?"

"That's the plan." Glory selected one of the hot macaroons and wondered when her mother had decided they were her favorite food. "It was such a relief to step into the apartment and back into my world. I actually wrote a chapter yesterday."

"You haven't been writing while you've been in California?"

Glory shook her head and swallowed a mouthful of macaroon. "I can't work there. The sun distracts me."

"Grandmom made some sweet things!" Damon catapulted himself into the kitchen and eyed the platter of cookies. "Oh, boy! Macaroons! My favorite!"

Like mother, like son, Glory thought as she gave Damon a nod when he positioned his hand over the platter. He grabbed two macaroons, then one more for good measure.

"Take some for Dani and Adam," Edna said with a delighted laugh. "Are you having fun playing outside, honey?"

Damon shrugged. "I miss the beach."

Glory stared at his "I Love New York" T-shirt. "Traitor," she said with a teasing snarl. "Believe it or not, New York has beaches, too."

"They're not the same." Damon grabbed three more macaroons. "They're dirty, and the water's cold. When are we going home?"

His question stunned Glory, and she was at a loss for an answer. She looked into his blue eyes and saw Wade in them.

"Glory, are you and Wade going to have more children?"

"What?" Glory blinked away the vision. "More children?" She looked at Damon, then back to her mother. "No."

"That's too bad. I've always thought large families were fun."

Glory threw Edna a bewildered glance. "Mother, if you thought large families were fun, why did you stop with me?"

"When are we going home?" Damon demanded.

"We *are* home!"

"I didn't say that I wanted a large family," Edna answered. "I just said I thought they seemed like fun."

"We're not home. Daddy's at home." Now Damon looked bewildered.

"Damon!" Glory took a deep breath and lowered her voice. "I'm talking to Grandmom. Why don't you go on outside and pretend you're in California?"

"Okay." He rounded his shoulders and dragged himself from the kitchen. Moments later the screen door slammed.

"Glory, what's wrong?" Edna covered one of Glory's hands with her own. "You're on edge. I think you've been drinking too much coffee. You've had three cups since you've been here."

"Mother, you sound like a commercial for decaffeinated coffee." Glory smiled, removing the sting from her words. "I just miss Wade."

"But you've only been away from him for three days!"

"I know." Glory moved her thumb along the top of her mother's hand. Age spots darkened the skin there, and Glory remembered when Edna's hands had been smooth and unblemished. "Mother, did you ever feel as if Daddy was drifting away from you?"

"Heavens, yes!" Edna patted Glory's hand reassuringly. "Every wife feels that way at least once during her marriage. It's normal, baby, but there's always a reason behind it. What's separating you and Wade?"

"The width of the United States."

"Oh, I think there's more to it than geography." Edna withdrew her hand from Glory's and reached for a macaroon. "I went to a free lecture the other day on two-career families. It was very interesting; I wish you could have been there with me to hear it."

"I don't need a lecture on that, Mother. I live it." Glory looked at the dregs in the bottom of her cup. She wanted more coffee, but she didn't want to hear about the dangers of caffeine according to Edna Mathers. She'd wait and then slip over to the coffee pot when her mother wasn't looking.

"This man—I think he was a psychiatrist—said that there's a great deal of stress and very little balance in a two-career family. It runs in cycles, you see." Edna stared at the macaroon in her hand as if it were a thesis. "For a while the husband's career might take precedence, then the wife's. It depends on the demands being made at any given time by each spouse's work."

"Hmmm. Tell me more." Glory eased from her chair and sidled behind Edna toward the percolator.

"He said that if one career begins to overshadow the other, then jealousies crop up. Those jealousies begin to eat away at the marriage."

Glory poured coffee into her cup. "Very interesting." She took a sip and glanced at her mother's back.

"That's number four, Glory."

Glory jumped slightly as if she'd been caught stealing. "I forgot that you had backward vision."

Edna laughed. "You get it when you deliver your first child. You have it, too."

"In more ways than one these days." Glory sat at the table and cradled the cup in her hands. "Lately I've been thinking about the past, when Wade and I were young and stupid and . . . blissfully happy."

"You were never stupid, and I doubt if you were ever blissfully happy." Edna brushed crumbs from her hands and pushed the platter of macaroons out of reach. "Are you sure you aren't pregnant?"

"Mother, Wade had a vasectomy, remember?"

"Oh, yes." Edna nodded, and a sad expression covered her face. "After the twins."

"Right."

"That's why you're not going to have any more children." Edna looked as if she'd stumbled across a telling clue in an Agatha Christie novel.

"Right again. It would be a dead giveaway to Wade that I was seeing another man."

Edna's eyes filled with horror. "Glory! You're not, are you?"

"Mother!" Glory rolled her eyes.

"Of course you're not!" Edna laughed, obviously relieved. "I've been watching those soap operas your father is so fond of, and I think they're making me crazy."

"Is Daddy still watching those things?"

"Yes. Daddy's still watching those things," Howard Mathers grumbled as he entered the kitchen and selected a glass from the cabinet.

Glory smiled, watching him with loving eyes as he poured milk into the glass. Suddenly she noticed that the skin around his neck was loose and that he had age spots on his forehead. When had he gotten old? she wondered with a twinge of dismay. When had he crossed the threshold from middle-ager to senior citizen?

"Want some macaroons?" Edna asked, lifting the platter from the table.

"Nope."

"They're your favorite!"

Howard looked at his wife as if she'd taken leave of her senses. "Never have been my favorite. They're Glory's favorite."

"Oh, that's right." Edna sighed and placed the platter back down on the table. "Father Time is playing tricks on me, Howard. The other day I couldn't remember how old I was. I had to look at my driver's license to be sure."

Howard chuckled and kissed Edna on the temple.

"Don't worry, Edna-love. It doesn't matter how old you are, just as long as you keep your sex appeal." He winked one green eye. "And you're a very sexy old broad."

"Howard!" Edna giggled like a girl. "Those soap operas are warping your brain!"

The love in their eyes brought a lump to Glory's throat. She thought of herself and Wade years from now, but the image was fuzzy. She couldn't quite imagine Wade with a pot belly and a bald head. And she didn't want to imagine herself with age spots and failing memory.

"Gotta go," her father announced as he walked toward the living room. " 'Days of Our Lives' is coming on."

"Are Julie and Doug still married?"

"Sure!" he looked pleased that Glory was interested in his favorite couple. "They're as happy as two bugs in a rug."

"What about Maggie and Micky?"

He frowned. "They're still married, but I think Maggie's ripe for an affair."

"What did I tell you?" Edna whispered when he'd left the room. Her index finger made circles near her ear. "Bats in the belfry. No wonder I'm losing my mind."

"You're not losing your mind, Mother," Glory assured her. "Just be thankful that he watches soap operas at home instead of living his own version with some other woman."

"You don't think Wade's having an affair, do you?" Horror was back in Edna's eyes.

"What is all this talk about affairs?" Glory asked, losing her patience. "Let's get on to another subject, okay?"

"Okay. Why are you jealous of Wade's career?"

"I'm not jealous of his career! I don't want to be a movie star."

"Glory, quit being so thickheaded." There was an edge

of impatience in Edna's voice. "You're having trouble adjusting to living with a busy, important man. It's that simple."

Glory scrutinized her mother over the rim of her cup. "Who said you were losing your mind?"

Edna gave her a sly smile. "I might forget trivial things, but not the important ones. And you and Wade are important to me. I know you've been having problems, and I think the reason rests with you, honey."

"So it's all my fault? Thanks, Mother. I could have gotten that from Wade's mother."

"Now, now. Don't go getting your back up." Edna gave her an I'm-your-mother look. "I'm not blaming you for anything; I'm simply pointing out that you're being selfish and you need to face it."

There's that word again, Glory thought with an inner moan. She finished her fourth cup of coffee and set her cup down with a thump. It was one thing to call yourself selfish, but it was quite another to hear it from your own mother.

"You had it all your way after you were married," Edna continued with infuriating persistence. "Now Wade's career is blooming, and you're faced with a husband who has work demands." A conspiratorial expression gleamed from her eyes. "You know, your father threw a fit when I joined the Gray Panthers and started taking night classes at the college."

"He did?"

Edna nodded, and her eyes twinkled. "I told him that I hadn't caused a fuss when he joined his company's bowling team or when he joined the Elks Club, so he could just put a sock in it!"

"You didn't!"

"I did!" She looked extremely proud of herself.

"Edna!" Howard's voice boomed from the living room.

"What?"

"Lucy Caulter's at the door!"

"Oh, pooh!" Edna pushed herself from the chair. "She's here for my notes from our 'Lady, Know Your Car' class. She had to miss last night because her daughter dumped the grandchildren on her. I'll be right back." She paused in the threshold and glanced over her shoulder. "Your father sulked for a few days, but he got over it. Like I always say, turnabout is fair play!"

Turnabout, fair play . . . Glory frowned. Had her mother been conspiring with Wade? She shook aside the notion, and her thoughts turned to that conversation with *Current* magazine that had upset her so. She should have been prepared for it, she told herself. After all, Wade's success hadn't evolved overnight, even though that's what those stupid gossip magazines said. No, it had come slowly— slowly enough for her to be aware of what was happening.

That first trip to California after his screen test had given her an inkling of things to come. He'd been treated like royalty. And when he'd returned from an interview with the director of *Tie-Breaker,* she'd known that something was up—and that it was big. From the expression he'd had on his face, she'd known that Wade Wilson was going to be more than just a name on her mailbox. For that point on, Wade Wilson was going to be the name of a star. He'd even said that himself, hadn't he? He'd stood there in the middle of that hotel room with its palm-tree wallpaper, an amazed expression on his face, a contract clutched in one hand, and told her without a shadow of a doubt . . .

" . . . this is it!" He waved the contract as if it were a banner. "This is our ticket to a better life, Glo! You're not looking at an unemployed actor—you're looking at Hollywood's next star!" A cunning smile curved his mouth. "How would you like to make love to a movie star?"

"Oh?" Glory looked around him. "Did you bring Robert Redford with you?"

Irritation pinched the skin around his eyes for a moment, and he held out the contract, pointing to a five-figure number. "Haven't you heard? Redford's moved over to make room for me. Look at that, Glo. That's more money than we've seen for quite a while."

Glory stared at the sum, and unrest stirred deep inside her. She looked up from the contract at the face of a movie star. "You're going to star in this picture?"

"I'm the leading man. Teresa Harper is starring. That's not bad company, is it?"

"No, considering her last leading man was already a superstar." Shock rattled her senses. "When do you start work?"

"The first of the month. We'll film here, so—"

"So we'll have to move here," Glory finished. "For how long? I'm in the middle of a book and—"

"Three months, that's all."

"Three months?" Glory's voice cracked. "We've got to live in Hollywood for three months?"

"You make it sound as if I just told you we were moving to Siberia!"

"Wade, I can't work here! I'm right in the middle of my next book, and you're asking me to pick up and move everything out here for three months. What about the kids? What about our apartment in New York? Where will we live? In this stinking hotel room?"

"Hey, hey!" He flung the contract onto the bed and grabbed her shoulders. "Will you listen to yourself?" His eyes darkened to that midnight blue that spoke fathoms. "You're talking as if this is the end of the world, when in fact it's just the beginning. I came here thinking we could celebrate my first big break, and you act like Scrooge!" He released her, turning his back and running a hand through his dark curling hair.

Shame covered her in a heavy blanket. Glory quelled the misgivings and fear his news had provoked and went to stand behind him. She wrapped her arms about him, her hands moving up and down his chest.

"I'm sorry, Tiny Tim." She kissed his back. "You just took me by surprise, honey. Turn around and give us a Technicolor kiss."

He pivoted slowly in her arms, and his eyes reverted to that safe, clear sapphire. "It's going to be great, Glo. We're going to be so happy now."

His lips brushed hers, then swooped for a deeper kiss. *We're going to be happy now.* Those words penetrated her mind as Wade's tongue penetrated her mouth. I thought we were already happy, Glory mused, trying to respond to Wade's seductive caress. She was holding a budding movie star in her arms. How many times had she sat in darkened theaters and fantasized about a moment like this? She'd daydreamed of driving Robert Redford to distraction, of reducing Paul Newman to a mass of quivering longing. But never, never had she dreamed of making film star Wade Wilson crazy with desire. It had been a long time since she'd had any fantasies about Wade. In fact, he'd fallen so readily into her arms right from the start that there hadn't been any point in simply imagining it.

He moved her toward the bed, and they fell onto it, still tangled in each other's arms. Was the day coming when other women—total strangers—would have fantasies about her husband? Glory smiled at the ridiculous thought.

"Do you like that?"

Glory stared into Wade's eyes and realized that he

thought she was smiling from the feeling of his fingers on her taut nipples.

"Yes, I love it," she answered, preserving his ego. She began undressing him, and her irritation mounted as she found herself looking at his body with the eyes of a casting director. Would his body and face be mesmerizing up there on the big screen? Glory squeezed her eyes shut as the answer rose quickly from the depths of her soul. Oh, Lord! He would be all the rage! And where would that leave her? The wife of a sex symbol? The spouse of . . .

". . . and that's your fifth cup."

Glory jumped back into the present and stared at the cup of coffee she'd just poured. She glared at her mother.

"I'm a grown woman, Mother! I can drink fifty cups if I want!"

"Temper, temper!" Edna placed an arm around her daughter's shoulders. "I'm on your side, baby."

Baby. Glory slumped and plopped back into the kitchen chair. She would always be a baby to her mother. Would the twins always be her babies?

"I'm glad you don't dump the kids on me like Lucy's daughter does. She doesn't even warn Lucy ahead of time. She just shows up! I told Lucy that she should charge her baby-sitting fees." Edna poured the remainder of the coffee into the sink, removing the temptation from Glory.

"You told me when I got pregnant with Adam that you'd raised your own kid and had no intention of raising mine," Glory reminded her with a smile. "I took that to heart, Mother."

"You know I adore the kids." Edna rinsed out the coffee pot and set it to one side. "I'd be glad to take them with prior notice. It's just a matter of common courtesy."

"I understand."

"And I understand your problem." Edna sat beside Glory at the table, and her fingertips began to trace the swirls of gold in the yellow Formica. "You should be supportive of Wade's work, Glory. He never tried to direct your career, and you shouldn't try to direct his." She glanced up. "Common courtesy."

"I know." Glory sighed, wrestling with her uneasiness. "I just get this feeling that he's not entirely comfortable with the direction his career is taking."

"Let him deal with that." Edna's tone was stern. "He'll sort it out for himself." Her expression brightened. "Now tell me about Fiona Larkin. Is she a stuck-up, spoiled, vain woman who has slept her way to stardom?"

"Mother, you've been reading that tabloid again," Glory accused with a laugh.

"Your father buys it, and—well, I've glanced at it now and then." She leaned forward, her eyes sparkling with interest. "Well, is she? What does Wade think about her?"

Glory smiled. She loved gossiping about Wade.

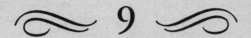

9

WADE UNFOLDED HIMSELF from the silver Ferrari, and
Glory could tell from the set of his shoulders that he was
dead tired. She turned from the window and glanced at
the wall clock. It was almost ten, and he'd been on the
movie set since seven that morning. He opened the front
door, and Glory greeted him with a kiss. He didn't even
bother to pucker.

"One of those days?"

"You said it." He dropped his briefcase onto the tiled
floor and headed for the kitchen. "I hope you saved
something for me. We had dinner, but it was the worst
quiche I've ever tasted."

"Real men don't eat quiche."

"What?" He looked at her as if she'd spoken in Rus-
sian.

"Nothing, just sit down. I saved some spaghetti sauce
for you, it'll only take a minute to boil the pasta."

"Are the kids asleep?"

"I put them to bed about a half-hour ago." Glory filled
a pot with water and set it on the burner. "You could go
in and give them good night kisses."

"I think I will. It seems I never get to see them these
days." He pushed himself away from the doorjamb and
walked toward the hallway.

Weariness was evident in every line of his body and
in his sluggish movements. Where was all the glitter and

glamour? Glory wondered as she added a pinch of salt to the water. No one had told them that being a movie star meant eighteen-hour days, six days a week. An ironic smile curved her mouth as she waited for the water to boil. Here she was, the wife of a movie star! What excitement! If only the writers for *Movie Analog* could see her now . . . "And here is glamorous Glory Mathers preparing warmed-over spaghetti for that sexy hunk, Wade Wilson . . ."

She chuckled at the whimsy. Life had an uncanny way of slapping you into the real world. Glitter faded. Glamour dulled. Warmed-over spaghetti was left.

"They're asleep." Wade flung himself into one of the chairs and rested his elbows on the dining table. Squeezing his eyes shut, he massaged his temples. "This was one of those hurry-up-and-wait days, thanks to Miss Glamour Puss."

"Miss Glamour Puss? Is that what you call Fiona these days?"

"That's what the crew calls her behind her back. The producer ordered a new trailer for her today. Fiona threw a fit and said she wouldn't work until they delivered a larger trailer to the set for her." He opened his eyes and looked at Glory. "Can you believe that she actually has a clause in her contract that specifies the size and type of trailer she's to have on the set?"

"I hope you don't start trying to keep up with the Larkins." Glory snapped the handful of long spaghetti in two and dropped it into the bubbling water.

"I don't give a damn about those things!" Wade drooped back into the chair with a disgusted sigh. "That's the big difference between New York and Hollywood. Hollywood actors are so caught up in status symbols— bigger trailers, top billing, chauffeured limos—none of which makes you a better actor. New York actors concentrate on their craft and could care less about the size of their dressing rooms." He plucked a napkin from the holder and began to shred it.

Glory contemplated lunging at the sounds of his discontent, but his next words silenced her.

"Arnold talked to Farleigh about that new play."

"He did?" Glory sat at the table beside Wade, forcibly containing her excitement. "What about it?"

"He's willing to consider me for the lead, but I'd have to audition."

":Is that good or bad?"

"Neither. It's just a slap in the face." His blue eyes became intense. "Bernard will sign me for his film without an audition. He likes my track record. I guess Farleigh isn't too impressed with my credentials."

"The film in Yugoslavia."

"Right."

Glory pursed her lips to keep from launching into a sales pitch for the Farleigh play. She stood and went to the stove to stir the pasta. Reminding herself of her resolution to let Wade conduct his own career, she fought to keep her opinions at bay. She busied herself with heating the sauce and pouring off the water from the prepared spaghetti, all the while reaffirming her decision to quit nagging Wade about films and Hollywood and sunny weather.

She'd returned from New York a week ago, determined to get herself and her marriage back on course. It was apparent that when things weren't right between her and Wade, nothing seemed right. Her writing suffered. She lost patience with the children. Even Peaches irritated her these days.

It was so good to be back, she thought with a contented smile. Back with Wade, she amended—not back in California. But something had been missing from New York,

and she'd discovered quickly that that something was
Wade. Even her prized friends couldn't erase the core
of loneliness in her.

Wade had met her and the kids at the airport, and
she'd known by the way his eyes lit up when he saw her
that she, too, had been sorely missed. They'd rushed
home, put Peaches in charge of the kids, and locked their
bedroom door. Making love had held a new significance.
They'd recaptured that sense of togetherness, and Glory
wasn't about to lose it again by harping on the Farleigh
play.

"You're awfully quiet," Wade observed as she set a
steaming plate of spaghetti before him. "Is something
wrong?"

"No." She poured iced tea into two glasses and handed
him one. "Your mother called this evening. She was
shocked when I told her you were still at work. I don't
think she believed me."

"I'll have to give her a call soon." He forked some
pasta and rolled his eyes with appreciation. "This looks
great. Thanks, honey."

"Is Fiona a good actress?"

"Pretty good," he answered around the mouthful.
"She'd be a lot better if she'd keep her mind on her work.
It takes *hours* to get her hair brushed just right and her
makeup perfect. She's really into looking great."

"Do you think she looks great?" Glory tried to sound
only mildly interested.

Wade shrugged. "I guess." His eyes widened. "But
her body is a lethal weapon. No kidding!" He took a
long swallow of the tea. "Her shoulder blades are like
knives. She's too thin."

"You can never be too thin in Hollywood." Glory
rested her chin in her hands. "I take it you've had experience with her shoulder blades."

A lopsided grin arrested his mouth. "We spent one whole day in bed that week you were in New York."

"Did she wear a body stocking?"

The grin took on force. "No. She wore...I think it was My Sin."

"How appropriate!"

He chuckled and tweaked her nose. "I love to bait you."

"There's something ludicrous about your business, Wade." She narrowed her eyes and scrutinized him as he wound spaghetti onto his fork.

His eyes twinkled at her observation, and white teeth glinted briefly with his quick smile. The critics were right: his expressions were priceless. Arnold, however, seemed to have settled on an asking price for them. It had been Wade's expressive face that had first appealed to her, coupled with that buoyant humor that was as much a part of him as was the shy dimple in his chin. Her discovery of his sensitivity and intelligence had branded her heart.

He paused in his attack on the pasta to roll up his shirtsleeves, and Glory switched her attention to the dark hairs that curled across his tanned forearms. The hair was similar in texture and color to that on his chest, and it peeved Glory to think that other women could view his body. It was small consolation knowing they could only look while she was allowed—and encouraged—to touch. Why couldn't he have a clause put in his contract that forbade any showing of skin below his neck?

"Are there any modest actors?" she asked.

"Nudity is just another costume to an actor, Glory."

"How does this nude scene differ from that porno film you were offered years ago?" She was unreasonably piqued.

He looked at her in shock. "There's all the difference

in the world! I mean, there's more to this film than just one bed scene after another. That porno film didn't require any talent from an actor."

"Oh." Glory shrugged. "I'm glad you see the difference."

He pushed aside his plate and took one of her hands in his. "Are you kidding me, or are you serious?"

"Half and half," she admitted, acknowledging the stirring of jealousy.

"I was only kidding you about the bed scenes, Glo. They're just a pain in the neck. It's all camera angles and bright lights." He raised her hand to his lips and kissed her fingertips. "We haven't had a chance to talk to each other since you've been back. How's your book going?"

"Pretty good." She thought of the blank page in her typewriter and winced. "I haven't done much on it since I've been back."

"Did I tell you that Arnold is jumping up and down about the reviews on *Miami Sundown?*"

She steeled herself. "Are they bad?"

"No!" Annoyance flickered in his eyes. "They're great, thank you very much."

"Sorry. My pessimism seems to be showing." She offered up a weak smile. "So tell me! How great are they?"

"Well, let me put it this way: start shopping for a gown to wear to the Academy Awards."

"Again?" Glory smiled, catching his bubbling exuberance. "Wade, these awards are getting so boring."

He laughed at her feigned ho-hum attitude. "It's the cross we must bear, darling," he said, matching her droll tone. "I suppose I'll be forced to buy a tux this year."

Glory giggled. "What are the critics saying about you?"

"Oh, that I'm hitting my stride and that I'm on my way to becoming *the* male box-office attraction." He made a dismissive gesture. "The usual stuff, you know." He cleared his throat dramatically and quoted, "Wade Wilson isn't just another pretty face, and he proves it in his latest film, *Miami Sundown*. Through sheer talent, he turns a mediocre film script into dynamite. Wilson can say more with the lift of an eyebrow than most actors can with pages of script." He sighed. "That sort of thing."

Glory squeezed his hand. "I always knew that eyebrow had star quality."

Wade examined her for long, searching seconds. "It's been some time since I've seen your eyes sparkle, Glo. Did that trip to New York lift your spirits?"

"Yes," she lied, recalling the nights she'd tossed and turned in that bed that had seemed so empty without Wade and those hours that had seemed like days. She'd gone to New York for tranquillity; but she'd found only loneliness. "Are you going to audition for Farleigh?" The question popped out, and she realized that it had been burning a hole in her tongue.

A cloud passed over his face, killing the light in his eyes. "I don't know. It bugs me that he wants me to audition. I'm going to sleep on it."

Glory glanced at the clock. "Speaking of sleep, I guess we'd better turn in."

"I've got some blue pages to look over before I go to bed." He pushed himself from the chair and retrieved his briefcase. "They're doctoring the script again."

"Who's rewriting it now? The producer? The director? The camera man?" She gathered the dirty dishes, her sharp movements matching the razor edge in her voice. Blue pages! Hollywood's way of sticking it to writers.

"The director has made some of the changes." He paused, as if finding it difficult to finish. "Fiona asked for the other rewrites."

"Fiona!" Glory dumped the dishes into the sink and pivoted to face Wade. "Fiona Larkin is a writer now?"

When Wade shrugged helplessly, Glory turned back to the sink and began rinsing the dishes and placing them in the dishwasher. "The gall of actors never ceases to amaze me. What do the writers have to say about these script changes?"

"I don't suppose they're happy about them, but there isn't much they can do about the situation. It's in their contract that—"

"That everyone from the Best Boy to the leading lady can rewrite their script," Glory finished for him. "I wouldn't sign a contract with a film company even if they offered me a million dollars and threw in Rhode Island to boot."

The telephone shrilled, cutting into Glory's tirade. Wade answered it while Glory started the dishwasher.

"It's for you. Penny." He handed the receiver to her. "Why don't you leave those dishes for Peaches? She is still on the payroll, isn't she?"

"It's hard to let go of my middle-class background. I keep forgetting I have a maid." Glory settled herself in one of the dining-room chairs. "Hello?"

"It's late, I know."

"That's okay, Penny. I'm still up. Is something wrong?" Glory waved at Wade as he disappeared into the living room.

"Something's right for a change." Penny sounded excited. "I just got word this afternoon that your book's been bought on a partial, and the editors are waiting for the rest of it. Can you finish it by January?"

"You're kidding."

"You can't finish by January? That gives you almost six months and—"

"No, no." Glory interrupted her. "I mean, you're kidding that you sold the book on a partial."

"I'm not kidding. Why are you so surprised? I hate to break the news to you, honey, but you're a best-selling author, and publishers like your work."

Glory sighed and wondered if she'd ever gain self-confidence in her writing. Every sale still astounded her. Every autograph-signing party intimidated her. "January?" She said the word through her stupor.

"Yes. I'll be sending you the contracts—and sit down before you read them. The advance they're offering is going to knock your socks off. Can you finish it by January? They need to know so they can put that into the contract."

"Yes, I guess I can, but—"

"Good. There's something else."

"What?"

"Are you sitting down?"

Glory gripped the receiver more tightly. "Yes."

"A film company is interested in negotiating for rights on this one."

Pressure. It began building within her as if she were a huge pressure cooker. Glory took a deep breath as an image of the top of her head popping off to allow steam to escape twisted into her mind.

"They want to make a film from my book?"

"That's the picture," Penny punned, sounding as if she were on the edge of bliss. "This has been one crazy day, Glory! It's as if publishing row and Hollywood just discovered what you and I have known all along—you're one talented lady."

"Blue pages."

"What?"

Glory shook her head and tried to form an intelligent sentence. "Hold off on the movie deal, Penny."

"Why?" Penny's voice crackled with confusion.

"I . . . just want to think about it."

"For how long?"

"Oh, how does a lifetime sound to you?"

"Glory!"

"I'm kidding," Glory consoled her, then wondered if she wasn't serious. "I can't make snap decisions. Tell them I can finish the book by the end of January, and send me the contracts. As for that movie business, let's just mull it over for a few weeks."

"A few weeks?" Penny's sigh of frustration breathed across the telephone lines. "Why drag your feet on this?"

"Please, Penny? Just a few weeks for me to get used to the idea." The pressure was building. The needle was swinging toward the red zone.

"Okay. I'll send those contracts, and we'll talk again in a couple of weeks. Is everything okay in Hollywood?"

"Everything's fine. I'll talk to you soon. Good-bye."

"Good-bye, honey. Take care of yourself."

Glory replaced the receiver. Blue pages. The words circled in her mind. It was silly to get so steamed over something like this, she told herself. The deal would probably fall through, and she'd have nothing to worry about. Worry about? Was a film deal something to worry about? A few years ago she would have been phoning everyone she remotely knew to tell them of her good fortune.

"What did Penny want?"

She looked up. Wade had entered the kitchen. He held a few sheets of blue paper in his hand.

"She just sold my book on a partial."

"Great!" He looked pleased as he bent to give her a congratulatory kiss. "This is the one about a mother, daughter, and granddaughter who live together?"

"Yes. I have to finish it by January."

"You'll do it." He poured tea into his empty glass. "What's the name of it?"

"*Women Scorned*. A film company is interested in buying rights to it."

The glass that was traveling toward his mouth froze

in mid-air, and Wade's fingers convulsed around it.
"Which film company?"

"I don't know." Glory's eyes widened. "I forgot to
ask."

He placed the glass and the blue pages on the table
and cradled her face in his hands. "Congratulations,
honey. I'm proud of you." His lips caressed hers but
received no response. He gazed deeply into her green
eyes. "What's wrong?"

"I'm not crazy about the idea of selling my work to
a film company and watching them butcher it."

"They won't butcher it. You're a good writer."

"And they aren't?" Glory pointed to the blue pages
on the table. "You told me they were the best in the
business."

"They are." He straightened, and his hands slid from
her face. "Everything can be improved."

"By the likes of Fiona Larkin? Don't make me laugh."
Mounting rage pushed her from the chair. "I'd rather die
than let a star get his or her hands on my work. Look
what Hollywood did to Scott Fitzgerald!"

The planes of his face hardened. "You're back on that
damned high horse again, Glory, and I'm not in the mood
to suffer through it." He grabbed the script pages and
pivoted sharply away from her.

"Wade, I didn't mean to include you in that—"

"I'm part of the film industry, Glory." His eyes burned
with anger as he turned back to her. "I know you think
we're a bunch of no-talent hustlers. You've made that
perfectly clear."

"No, not you!" Glory touched his forearm, but he
jerked back from her.

"You've got this prejudice against anything that has
to do with Hollywood, and you expect me to share in it,
but I won't! You're determined to hate everything about

this industry, and for the life of me I don't understand why. What's it ever done to you except make your life easier?"

"It's made *your* life easier, not mine."

An incredulous laugh burst from him, and disappointment invaded his eyes. "You know, Glory, I wish you were just half as effective at handling my success as you were at handling my failure."

The steam of her anger escaped, and she stared at him for several moments as her body slumped in defeat. Tears stung her eyes, and she shouldered past him and walked blindly toward their bedroom. She didn't bother to turn on the lights but groped toward the bed and flung herself onto it. The tears felt good as they dampened her cheeks. She wanted to cry. She wanted to let the pressure ooze from her body and mind.

Words. A new batch of tears welled in her eyes. Words were her friends and her enemies. Sometimes they flowed from her like sweet honey, and other times they were acid-coated and ate through the fabric of her life, separating her from those she loved. She should have kept her mouth shut this time, she told herself. She should have kept those words about the film industry inside, where they couldn't hurt Wade.

But no. She'd had to blurt them out, and now she couldn't retrieve them. She couldn't repair the damage.

She undressed and slipped between the cool sheets. Wade had said she had been able to handle his failures but not his successes. Was there a germ of truth in that? she wondered as her eyelids grew heavy. There'd been many failures in those first years of their marriage, and she had handled them with remarkable ease. She'd even grown used to Wade's disappointments. They had been routine. Wade would audition, and he wouldn't get the part. There had been close calls, but he always seemed to come home empty-handed, and she'd been there to console him and to boost his sagging ego.

There had been borderline successes along the way, she remembered sleepily. Like that Off-Broadway play. Wade had been thrilled to be in rehearsals again, and he'd said he had a feeling that the play was destined for Broadway. Glory had dutifully attended the opening night—which had also been the closing night. Years later she could still feel his misery, his crushing loss. It had felt like a death in the family.

She opened her eyes and stared at the darkened room. It had been dark backstage that night. Shadows had lurked in every corner and upon every face. Everyone had talked in whispers, as if they were attending a wake. Sad expressions and eyes glistening with tears had greeted her as she made her way to the drab dressing room where Wade sat huddled before a dingy vanity. In the distance she had heard the wracking sobs of a woman—the leading lady? It was odd that she could remember little details, like the way the mirror on the vanity had been cloudy with grime and that several of the light bulbs around the mirror hadn't been working. Nothing had seemed to be working that night. She'd stared into the distorting mirror at her husband's bent head and drooping shoulders. A telegram of congratulations from his parents was crumpled in his hand, and Glory had felt her heart breaking for him. She had touched his shoulder, felt him tremble before he raised pain-filled eyes to meet hers in the mirror...

...and the sight shattered her heart and brought scalding tears to her eyes.

"It just isn't fair, Glo," he whispered. "It just isn't fair to work so hard to be good, and then they don't even give you a chance to show your stuff."

"I thought you were wonderful in the play, Wade." She pulled a rickety chair closer to him and sat down.

"I can't understand why they closed the show."

"They closed it because it stinks." He brushed his dusky hair back with his hands. "It felt so good in rehearsals, and it just fell apart tonight. I don't understand it. I could feel the play breaking up"—he tore the telegram in half—"but I couldn't do anything about it."

"You did your best." Glory leaned her cheek against his slumped shoulder. "Put this one behind you. The next play will be—"

"Don't talk to me about the next play, Glory." There was a biting edge to his voice. "I haven't accepted the death of this one yet."

Glory watched as he made confetti out of the telegram. "Would you like to go out and lift a few mugs with a married lady?"

"I don't know." He wiped a hand over his face, then stared at the streaks of makeup on his palm.

"Come on," Glory urged, tugging on his arm. "If you're lucky, you might lure me into bed—and I hear that married women are great lovers."

"Is that what you hear?"

"That's what they tell me."

He drew a deep breath and reached for a jar of cleansing cream. "Let me get this stupid makeup off, and we'll get out of this morgue."

"Now you're talking, big boy."

They left the dark theater for the gaudiness of a bar. Selecting a table in a secluded corner, they ordered mugs of brew and chomped on pretzels and peanuts. A popular blues singer wailed from the jukebox about lost love and a man who'd done her wrong.

"I'd cry into my beer, but that's so clichéd." The atmosphere was weaving melancholy and regret into Wade's blue eyes. "Don't you ever get tired of watching me fail?"

"Stop with the self-pity, Wilson." Glory smiled and

lifted her mug. "To the next play starring Wade Wilson."

"Amend that to the next play offering Wade Wilson a job, and I'll honor it. At this point I'm not interested in starring; I'm just interested in working."

"*Salut!*" Glory tapped his mug with her own and took a sip of the tart beer. Mindful that her usual tactics weren't working, she reached deeper into her bag of tricks. How could she dispel that look of defeat from his face? This time was different. She couldn't begin to empathize with the pain he was experiencing. Sure, she'd gathered her share of rejections, but she'd never experienced this soul-crushing disappointment that was reflected in his dark blue eyes. Feminine tricks wouldn't do now. He was way beyond such nonsense. He was in some deep, dark corner she couldn't reach.

Wade ran a hand along his jaw, which was sandpapery with tomorrow's whiskers. Slowly a grim determination set his jaw and invaded his eyes.

"I guess I'll start making the rounds again." He squared his shoulders with considerable effort and stared into the mug. "Commercials, soap operas, automobile shows. If nothing clicks in the next few months, I'll check out the waiter jobs."

"Something will click." Glory smiled her encouragement, but Wade frowned it aside.

"I know you mean well, Glo, but your cheery attitude is grating on my nerves. You're already planning tomorrow, and I'm still stuck on today."

"Unstick yourself. Don't look back, Wade. Look forward!"

A grim smile stretched across his lips. "You never give up, do you? You'd make a great cheerleader."

"I'm your biggest fan, remember?"

"Yeah." He took a long swallow of the beer. "Do me a favor?"

"Anything."

"Stow the cheers for now. I want to listen to the blues. I want to wallow in my misery. God knows, I deserve it."

"Wade," Glory pleaded, her fingers wrapping around his wrist. "I hate to see you like this. Smile for me."

"Later." He disengaged himself from her clinging fingers and finished the beer. The barmaid supplied a refill, and Wade lapsed into a gloomy silence. The blues filled the air, and a siren outside moaned of bad news. Death hovered in the air, and Wade seemed content with it.

Glory watched him go from tipsy to looped. With each beer he seemed to pull himself up, rung by rung, to a numbed good humor. It rankled her that he chose Budweiser over her.

Dawn was breaking as they walked home, and Wade stopped at a newsstand to buy a couple of papers. Each gave cursory reviews of the play, but one critic pointed out that ". . . in spite of a horrendous script and horrible direction, a few of the actors showed promise. Wade Wilson, in particular, tried to rise above the ashes with noble effort."

"I'm going to send that critic a dozen roses tomorrow . . . uh . . . today," Wade said as he tucked the newspapers under his arm. His smile was lopsided, and his words were a trifle slurred.

Glory linked her arm in his, partly to steady him. He was feeling no pain. "Let's get you home."

"Is this the part where we make love?"

"When we get home, yes."

"Good. This is my favorite part."

They stumbled home, but there was no lovemaking. Wade was out like a light by the time Glory got him into bed. She closed the blinds against the sun and looked at Wade with loving eyes. Her hands covered her stomach where a fetus nestled.

Wade had suffered tonight. His sense of humor and his optimism had deserted him, leaving liquor as a last resort. The days ahead would be dreary. No more rehearsals. No more waiting for opening night. He'd start making those endless rounds of auditions that made her marvel at his stamina.

Glory slipped into bed beside him, curving herself against his warm body. He stirred and struggled to consciousness.

"Did we make love?"

Glory smiled and pressed a kiss on his shoulder. "Yes," she fibbed.

"Was I good?"

"You were great."

A satisfied grin curved his mouth. "I thought so." His eyes sparkled briefly, signalling the return of his good nature, and he...

...entered the bedroom. Glory tensed. She kept her eyes closed, listening as he undressed. Where had that sense of humor gone? she wondered. Was it still there? Or had years of disappointments and broken promises destroyed it? The sound of the shower drifted to her. She fought the urge to join him in the tub and try to tease him into a good mood. Something told her that he didn't want to be in a good mood. He wanted to be mad at her. And maybe he deserved to be angry.

Was she trying to detour him from his destiny? How long could she keep constructing barriers before he got fed up and lost his patience?

Knowing that he would soon finish his shower and come to bed, only to turn an indifferent back to her, Glory left the bed and wandered into the living room. Breakers were pounding relentlessly at the shore, and the ocean looked black and cruel.

Glory wrapped an afghan around her and stared at the fury outside while she contemplated the restlessness within her.

She lifted her gaze to the blinking stars and remembered reading astrological charts on herself and Wade. Was there something to all that mumbo-jumbo? Her characteristics had included drive, determination, ambition, and a total lack of tact. The astrologer had written that she would plod along like a sure-footed goat and that each step would be carefully calculated. She didn't like surprises, and she had no time for people who were without clearly defined goals.

Wade's characteristics included impulsiveness, forcefulness, a supreme ego, and a strong sense of self-worth. He showed a surprising combination of idealism and realism, and a way of speaking his mind without being tactless. His pride was his most valued quality, and once he was stripped of it, he was a fallen man.

The astrologer had written that their Capricorn/Aries union had a good chance at success. Wade would dilute Glory's tactless approach to others, and Glory would stand behind Wade through thick and thin. The road might be rocky, but each was determined and stubborn. They both took commitments to heart and would rather die then renege on sacred vows.

Problem areas, according to the astrologer, revolved around goals and careers. Glory was a take-charge person, a born leader. Wade had the same characteristics. The astrologer suggested that they always be aware of each other's need to lead and realize that there would be occasions when one of them would be forced to follow.

The star Glory was gazing at suddenly seemed to take on intensity and crystallize her thoughts. Follow...? She tipped her head to one side. Wade had been following her for years, and now he was trying to lead. Was she fighting that tooth-and-nail for her own selfish reasons? And did those reasons have absolutely nothing to do with Wade's ultimate happiness?

Recalling her mother's mention of a two-career family, Glory wondered if she'd ever really experienced such a thing. She'd always thought she was involved in a two-career marriage, but Wade's career had, until recently, been a shadow. Was she resenting Wade's intrusion into her role as breadwinner? Was the ram overtaking the goat?

Glory closed her eyes on a sigh. It was silly to try to find solutions in the stars. The solution could only be found within herself. This restlessness no doubt stemmed from the demands Wade's career was making on her life. She wanted him to achieve his goal, just as she'd achieved hers. But he'd forgotten his goal. His goal had been Broadway, not films! How could he be satisfied with blue pages and palm trees when Broadway beckoned with marquees and opening nights?

That pesky inner voice chided her again. It was his career. That's what Penny and her mother kept telling her. Why didn't she listen? They were right. He'd never interfered in her career decisions. He'd just . . . just gone along for the ride. She winced and hugged the afghan closer to her shivering body. What had that done to his pride? That precious pride of his that was his very backbone? He'd bled silently, and she'd been oblivious, for the most part, to his excruciating pain.

She'd just have to stick to her vow of silence on the subject of Wade's career, she told herself. It went against her grain, but it seemed to be the only solution for the time being. With a little luck, everything would work out, and they'd be back in New York by fall.

Glory pulled herself up short, her body tensing. She was doing it again! Thinking of herself and not of Wade.

But that Broadway show would be a tremendous boost to his career, wouldn't it? So it wasn't selfish to hope that they'd return to New York.

With a tortured moan, Glory turned away from the sight of the raging ocean and picked her way through the living room and up the stairs. In the dim light from a million stars, she could see Wade's back. She let the afghan fall to the floor, and she slipped into bed beside him. He didn't stir. He didn't roll over and welcome her into his arms. The ram wasn't his usual forgiving self.

Glory stared at his imposing back and curled her hands into fists to keep from running her fingertips longingly down his spine. It seemed that a gaping ravine separated them instead of only a few inches of pastel sheet. And the goat didn't have the strength to jump that ravine. Glory closed her eyes and rolled into a dream.

She dreamed of the bright lights on Broadway. She was walking along a street in the theater district, and she was pulling Wade along behind her. He was resisting. Finally she pivoted to face him.

"Come on! You've always wanted this. Follow me," she yelled above the din of traffic.

"I don't want to follow you there. I want to lead you there." He whispered the words, but she heard them clearly. "I want to find my own way. I don't need you as a guide."

He ripped his hand from hers, and a mist obscured him for a moment. When the mist cleared, he was gone. Glory turned in circles, looking for him. A blinking marquee captured her attention. *WADE WILSON APPEARING IN I Love Los Angeles*.

"No! No! It messes up my life. You can't love Los Angeles!" she screamed at the marquee.

Eerily, Wade's face appeared over the marquee like a scene from *The Wizard of Oz*. He shook his head regretfully.

"Sorry, Glo. You'll have to follow. It's my turn to lead."

The dream dissolved, and Glory struggled to wakefulness. She glanced at the clock and closed her eyes again. Two more hours before the alarm, she thought sleepily. How would she handle tomorrow? Could she handle their tomorrows as skillfully as Wade had handled their yesterdays?

Wade stirred beside her and rolled to face her. Still asleep, he flung one arm across her stomach and fitted one muscular leg between hers. He murmured something in his sleep, and a grin tugged at one corner of his mouth.

Glory smiled. She loved sleeping with him.

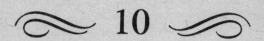

10

"YOU'VE FINISHED IT?"

"Yes." Glory sat back in the office chair with a relieved sigh. Satisfaction swept through her like a cool summer breeze, promising that everything would be coming up roses. She laced her hands across her stomach and glanced from her typewriter to Peaches. "It's finished. Penny will be flabbergasted." She laughed, a carefree, wonderful sound. "What am I talking about? *I'm* flabbergasted! I've never written so fast and so effortlessly." She gave Peaches a sly wink. "I've got a good feeling about this book. Everything about it makes my brain tingle."

"Good." Peaches flopped into a chair and folded her hands atop a cardboard box in her lap. "You can start helping me rewrite my book now."

"Peaches, I can't do that." Glory inched herself up to a straight-backed position. "I've told you that I've done everything I can for you. I can't write your book. *You've* got to write it." Glory placed her hand on the final page of her own manuscript. "I didn't have to finish this until January, and here it is only August. Amazing, isn't it?" She turned her wondering eyes on Peaches' irritable expression.

"Yeah, now let's talk about my book. I don't know how to rewrite. You're gonna have to show me." She lifted the lid of the box. "Take this first page where you—"

"Read my lips, Peaches." Glory leaned forward a bit. "No."

"You wrote all these squiggly marks on it, and I don't know what they mean!" Peaches flung out her skinny arms in desperation. "This one here looks like a pig's tail—it's all over the place!—what's that mean?"

Glory glanced at the first page in the box. "It means to delete—take it out." She settled back in the chair and crossed her legs beneath her. "Do what I did, Peaches. Take some courses in writing and learn your trade. That is, if you're really serious about this book."

"I'm serious!" Peaches' dark eyes glinted with the challenge.

"Good. Do you think a person who wants to be a sculptor just picks up a mallet and starts hammering away at a piece of rock? No. You take courses and read textbooks and experiment until you get the hang of it. Writers, too."

"You said this was promising!"

"It is promising. You have innate talent and determination. Now you must learn your trade."

"How am I going to take classes on my wages?" Peaches scoffed.

"You can afford it." Glory gathered the wayward pages on her desk. "You're making more money than I was when I started college."

"I couldn't go back to school. I'd flunk out."

"Peaches, you can excuse yourself from everything in life." Glory switched off her typewriter and sighed. "Believe me, I know what I'm talking about. I've seen many a fine writer—some of them much more talented than I am—make excuses for not writing, while other lesser talents"—Glory paused and pointed to herself—

"wrote and wrote and got published. Don't be one of these I'd-write-but people, Peaches."

"You won't help me write it?" Peaches asked, making one last attempt at twisting Glory's arm.

"No. I have my own writing to consume me." She stretched, looking forward to a long-distance call to Penny and the announcement of her astounding news. "Where are the kids?"

On cue, Adam bounded into the room. He came to a dead stop, his eyes wide. "Ooops! Sorry. Can I come in?"

"Yes." Glory held out her arms, eager to share her good mood. "Come here, you, and give your old mom a hug."

He wriggled in her embrace, twisting his head about to look at her. "Daddy's home. He just drove up."

"You're kidding!" Glory looked at her watch. "It's only two."

"Maybe he's finished the movie," Adam suggested as he removed himself from Glory's arms.

"No, he said he had a few more scenes to do." Glory untangled her legs and stood. "I hope nothing's wrong."

"Lucy, I'm home!" Wade called in his best Ricky Ricardo voice.

"In here!" Glory answered as Adam raced from the room. She heard the kids clamor for Wade's attention and smiled. They'd missed Wade these past few weeks; he was hardly ever home.

"Hello!" His smile told her that everything was fine. "Hey, Peaches! What's for dinner?"

"Dinner?" Peaches rose from the chair, clutching her cardboard box to her chest. "I don't think about dinner until five."

"Start thinking about it now. I've got a scene to shoot tonight, so we'll have an early dinner." Wade draped an arm about Glory's shoulders. "Excuse us, Peaches? I'm going to seduce my wife."

"Oh, brother!" Peaches chuckled and closed the door behind her.

"Such a charming woman," Wade observed with heavy sarcasm. "Two more scenes to shoot, and we wrap the film."

"Really?"

"Really. Tomorrow's our last day." He pulled her around into his arms. "It's looking good. Real good."

"I finished my novel today."

"Already?"

"Yes." Glory eased her arms about his waist, looping her thumbs in the waistband of his jeans. "It's the very best I've ever written. Once I got started, it just flowed. I wrote more in one month than I usually do in six."

"What was your inspiration?" Wade asked, rubbing his nose lightly against hers.

She hesitated. She couldn't tell him that her inspiration came from her inner frustration. Her writhing restlessness had fit so naturally into the tone of her novel that it had been a means of therapy. She'd released her feelings of helplessness onto the pages of her manuscript. The reason the book worked was because the emotions were so real they nearly jumped from the pages and grabbed one by the throat. But she couldn't tell Wade that. She was afraid he'd take it wrong. He'd think this was her newest tactic in making him feel guilty for taking her from old New York.

"Well?" His arms tightened. "Are you going to tell me, or keep it a secret?"

"I'll keep it a secret," she opted gratefully.

"What's his name?" Wade's brows lowered over eyes that gleamed with mischief.

"Talent. Incredible Talent. Do you know him?"

"We've met." Wade's lips trailed down her cheek to

the corner of her mouth. "Watch out, your ego's showing."

"I've got to let it out now and then." Her hands traced his shoulder blades beneath the knit shirt. "It's so nice to have you home in the daylight. How about a little afternoon delight?"

He chuckled into her hair. "Dessert first, dinner later. Is that it?"

"Why not?" Glory placed a finger to her lips. "We'll slip into the bedroom, lock the door, and let Peaches worry about dinner and the kids for a few hours."

"You're in a good mood, aren't you?" he asked as he followed her from the study and upstairs to their bedroom.

"Of course. I'm always in a good mood when I finish a book." She closed the bedroom door and smiled beguilingly at him. Sunlight poured over him, glancing off his black hair, firing his blue eyes, and adding a bronze color to his skin. One winged brow lifted, and the corners of his mouth twitched. "You look so cute." Her eyes moved slightly as she focused her senses on his towering virility.

"Cute?" He scowled. "Kids and puppies are cute." He placed his long-fingered hands at his waist. "Well, don't just stand there. Jump on my bones!"

With a laugh, Glory tackled him, and they fell backward onto the bed. She gave him a quick, hard kiss. "I love you."

"Ditto." His fingers began weaving through her hair. "I've decided to audition for Farleigh."

The news sent a spiraling euphoria through her, but she kept it from surfacing. She managed a noncommittal lift of her eyebrows.

"Oh? Are you sure that's what you want to do?" She held her breath and waited for his answer.

"Yes, for now. We'll just see how it goes. If I get

lucky and am cast in the play, it would be quite a plum."

"Quite." She began inching his knit shirt up over his stomach. "What about Bernard?"

"He'll wait. If I don't get the play, then I'll talk business with him."

A knock sounded at the door, and Glory matched Wade's frown.

"Yes, Peaches?" Glory called, recognizing the brisk rapping of knuckles.

"You guys gonna be holed up in there all afternoon or what?" Peaches voice was like fingernails scratching a blackboard.

"We're going to be busy for a while!" Wade propped himself on his elbows and glared past Glory's shoulder at the door. "Take care of the kids and start dinner, okay?"

"Do I have a choice?" Peaches rejoined with her usual sharp tongue.

"You could quit."

"Wade!" Glory whispered, slapping his shoulder playfully.

"Don't tempt me!"

Glory pressed her knuckles to her mouth to keep her giggles silenced until she was sure Peaches had walked away from the door. "Wade, you'd better be careful. Someday she's going to take you up on that and quit," she warned between bursts of laughter.

"She loves to quarrel, and she'll never find better sparring partners—and she knows it." Wade glanced down at the hem of his shirt, which was gathered just under his arms. "Now where were we?"

"Right here." Glory moved her lips against his chest, and her fingers rasped through the curling hair there.

With practiced ease, she undressed Wade, and then he undressed her. Feeling free of their burdens, they tossed their clothes about the room with wild abandon. Sunlight streamed through the windows, bathing them in amber. Glory traced the lines of Wade's body, paying closer attention to them than she had in some time. He was really in fine shape, she mused as she pressed tiny kisses across his flat stomach while her fingers kneaded the taut muscles in his thighs.

His body hadn't changed in the years they'd been together, and Glory wondered if he felt the same about hers. The tip of her tongue flicked the skin just below his navel, and she looked up to find his eyes. They told her that they were pleased with what they saw.

"Do I look the same as the day you married me?" she asked in a whisper, immediately wondering if it were wise to place dynamite in his hands.

He screwed up one eye in thoughtful contemplation. "No. You wore a dress that day, didn't you? White, I believe?"

"You know what I mean." Glory gripped his thighs and used them to push herself up his body until her lips were poised above his. "Have I gained weight or lost weight or . . . changed in any physical way?"

"You've gotten more lovable." His hands rested lightly on the small of her back. "Physically, you're more beautiful now than you were then."

"I've gotten better?" Glory asked, a bit dubious.

"To these old eyes, you have. What about me? Have I changed?"

Glory caressed his cheeks with the backs of her hands. "You're lovely."

"Honey, for a writer you have a terrible vocabulary. Men aren't cute or lovely."

"You are." Glory laughed softly as her love for him swelled within her. "You defy description."

"Ah, that's better." Wade's hands slid up her back as

his mouth fastened on hers. His lips and tongue were as relentless as the waves crashing against the shore outside.

Glory caressed him, her slower pace forcing him to match it. His kiss became less urgent and more tender. She wanted this interlude to stretch into hours. The novel was finished. The audition was set. New York didn't seem so far away now. What better way to cap a day of accomplishment than in making love with the man who had captured her heart so many years ago?

Wade rolled her onto her back, and his lips and tongue teased her soft breasts until their peaks were flushed and firm. He settled her more completely beneath him with hands that lingered and loved. Sun rays played across his rippling shoulders and hips, and she traced their patterns with her fingertips. His mouth left moist circles on her skin as it traveled from her breasts down her body to her ankles. He sat back on his haunches, one of her ankles held in his hands, and began to massage her calf. His eyes met hers and transmitted a message of joyous appreciation.

"I love bed scenes." He grinned and ran his fingertip along the sole of her foot.

Glory jerked in an involuntary reaction. "Don't tickle," she pleaded. She didn't want this lazy mood to dissolve into fits of giggles.

His lips replaced his finger, and Glory curled her toes and sighed expansively. Massaging fingers moved slowly up her leg to the inside of her thigh. Glory arched her back, and a flash of passion burst through her, sending tingles down the length of her body. Wade murmured something unintelligible. Fingers and tongue sought her out, drawing forth the essence of her femininity. Her hands fell to his head, and she pressed him closer.

Wade made love as if he had invented it. His passion and expertise consumed her, transforming her into a writhing solar flare. He slipped inside of her easily, and Glory wrapped her legs against his broad back. She wanted to hold him there, lock him to her forever. When he was good, he was beyond belief.

He seemed content just to remain still and feel her clutching at him as if he were the brass ring on a carousel. Glory's lashes fluttered, giving her a hazy view of him. He was a portrait of ecstasy. In his face she saw the beauty of love, the vulnerability of commitment, and the comfort of possession. She thought of all the nights she had made love with him, and yet she'd never stopped to really examine this private expression on his face. Yes, private. No other woman could see this expression of exquisite anticipation. He might fake it for the director and for all those strangers who sat in darkened theaters, but this was the real thing in front of her. This was a Wade Wilson who belonged entirely to Glory Mathers.

The dark fringe of his lashes lifted to reveal glistening pools of pastel blue. A tiny smile touched the corners of his mouth.

"Feels so good, doesn't it?" he murmured.

"Yes. I wouldn't mind being cast in bronze."

He broke off his chuckle abruptly. "Don't make me laugh," he begged hoarsely. "I'll lose it, and I don't want to lose it now." He moved slightly, circling before he withdrew. Taking a deep breath, he came to her again.

"Wade, Wade," she whispered, all other words eluding her. She balanced herself carefully as he pulled her up until her hips rested on his thighs. His arms slid under her back, and he lifted her until she was sitting on his lap, her arms wound about his neck. "Cuddle me. I love it when you cuddle me."

He buried his face in the side of her neck and held her as if there were no tomorrow. He quivered deep within her, and Glory knew she could not keep him immobile for much longer. She relented and let him tumble her to the bed. His body was a blanket of warm skin upon hers.

A cloud passed over the sun, throwing the room into gray shadows. Wade's eyes burned feverishly through the grayness as his body plunged into hers. His roving mouth created a light of its own, spilling golden rays throughout her body.

Just as the sun rid itself of the cloud, they reached their zenith. Like a brush fire, their passion raced through them, Glory panted for a decent breath while the world flared around her.

Soon lazy lips nudged hers in a kiss that was devoid of strength. Glory laughed softly and wove her fingers in the curls of Wade's hair. "You're not finished, are you? I was just getting warmed up."

He lifted his head and arched an eyebrow. "Ungrateful wretch! I'll teach you!"

His tickling fingers drove her to a quick surrender. "I'm grateful! I'm grateful!" she managed between giggles. She brushed aside his hands and rained kisses across his breastbone. "I'm soooo grateful," she purred before lightly sinking her teeth into his flesh.

"You're an animal." Wade glanced at the small indentations her teeth had left on his shoulder. "I hope I bruise so I can show it to the guys tonight."

She laughed with him. He rolled onto his side, and she instinctively fitted her curves to his contours.

"I'll be glad when the film's finished," she admitted after a few minutes of reflection.

"So will I. It'll be nice to say, 'It's been real, and it's been fun, but it hasn't been real fun,' to Miss Glamour Puss."

Glory traced the swirl of hair on his chest with her fingertip. "You know, I was kind of jealous of Fiona for a while."

He tensed, and she could feel him glaring down at the top of her head. "Jealous of Fiona? That's ridiculous! Didn't you know that she irritates the stuffing out of me?"

"Well, she seems to fit in so well here in California." Glory snuggled closer, keeping her gaze pinned to her roving fingertip. "I felt like a wallflower around her and . . . and I thought you might like her Hollywood style."

"Hollywood," he snarled. "I've just about had it with Hollywood. If I do any other films, I'd like to find a house away from Rodeo Drive and Beverly Hills." He hugged her closer. "I like Malibu, but it grates on me after a while. Maybe we could find a house surrounded by several acres—outside Los Angeles—with a small school system. I'll check around."

"What about Farleigh?" Glory reminded him as panic erupted. Had he already changed his mind about the New York audition?

"I can't bank on that." He was quiet for several moments. "Besides, chances are I'll be back here eventually to make more films. Once *Twisting Turns* is released, I have a feeling my stock option is going to burst through the ceiling."

"Mmmm." *Keep your mouth shut! Keep your mouth shut!* Glory repeated the warning to herself over and over until the urge to launch into an ode to New York City abated. She wanted to keep the good times rolling. It was so nice being here in his arms and tangling her legs with his. "I want us to be this happy always, Wade." She raised her head a little to look into his eyes. "We've been distant lately. I was scared that we'd become strangers to one another."

"Glory," he chided her before placing a kiss on her forehead, "that won't ever happen. We can always reach out to one another." He laid his head back on the pillow and stared at the ceiling light. "Remember that time you got raving mad at me because I criticized your book? It was that second book. The one that got the lousy reviews."

"Talking Heads," she supplied.

"Yes, that's the one."

"Why is it that I can remember every name of every production you've ever been in, and you can't remember the names of my novels?"

"You didn't give me time to remember." He shifted slightly, throwing one leg over hers. "Anyway, that was a bad time for us. There was a lot of pressure . . . I'd just lost a part in something or other—"

"Thompson's made-for-television adaptation of *Our Town*." Glory sighed, pressing her point. It was silly that this characteristic of his irritated her so. It was like squeezing toothpaste tubes in the middle. Minor, but a flash point nonetheless.

"Right, and you were pregnant with the twins, and your book was awful."

"Bite your tongue, Wilson, before I do it for you."

"Okay," he amended, "it wasn't awful. It just wasn't very good."

Glory started counting to ten.

"I can't pinpoint what actually brought the argument about—"

"I broke one of Penny's cardinal rules."

He chuckled. "Which one?"

"Never ask your mother or husband to comment on anything you write," Glory quoted as she propped herself on one elbow and looked at Wade's near-perfect profile. "I asked you to read the book and give me your opinion. Of course, I expected a glowing review from my loving husband, not a carefully conducted massacre."

"I was getting back at you for editing my love poem." He slanted his gaze at her. "And it wasn't a massacre."

"Wade, if you had just said, 'It's okay,' it would have seemed like a massacre, coming from you." She smiled, recalling that afternoon when he'd finished reading her book and she'd demanded his opinion of it. She'd done some stupid things in her life, but that took first prize.

"I should have taken the Fifth." Wade yawned and stretched like some great jungle cat. "The point is that we got through those hurt feelings and thoughtless words. We always bounce back..." His voice trailed off, and his lashes rested darkly against his skin.

Glory contemplated his example as she watched him slip into a dream. Funny he should remember that time as a rocky patch in their marriage. Had it been that climactic? True, they'd both been under pressure, and she hadn't really bargained on his telling the truth. She should have known better. Wade never lied. His honesty had taught her a lesson. She'd broken one of Penny's rules, and she'd learned never to break another one.

Penny was right. It was bad enough to be criticized by strangers. Like that witch at the last autograph party in...Dallas? Or was it Houston? Wherever it was, it was imprinted on her memory for life. The witch had elbowed her way to the card table where Glory was signing books and had asked in a voice that would have made a train conductor green with envy, "Is this book better than your last one?"

Glory had gazed at her in shock for a few moments. Didn't this woman understand that her question was like asking her if she liked Damon better than Dani? Finally she'd managed, "I wouldn't say that it's *better* than my last one—"

"Well, I don't want it then. I couldn't stand your last one."

That unfeeling comment had ruined the remainder of the book-signing party. Instead of greeting her admirers with a smile, Glory couldn't help but cringe from them and adjust her armor in anticipation of the next attack on her fragile ego.

Wade's criticism had cut even deeper. It had gone past her ego to her heart.

But *Talking Heads* had taught her a lesson. She had made a name for herself as a writer who could entertain and educate readers about women's concerns without preaching. In *Talking Heads* she had detoured from her style, and instead of having a woman as the main character, she'd written it from a male point of view. That had been a mistake. But she hadn't been able to see her own faults in the book—not until Wade pointed them out. Hmmm. Maybe Penny was wrong. Maybe Wade was an exception to the rule. He'd helped her—despite herself—that time. He was an actor, and he knew a good story when he saw one. He'd proved that when she'd finally forced him to critique her book.

Glory fell back onto the pillow and plucked at the memory. She'd licked her wounds and circled him for days like an injured mongrel who needed sustenance but didn't trust the man who offered it. However, his critical remarks began to eat through her distrust. Some of his comments had a ring of truth to them, and she found herself wanting a more thorough explanation of his opinions. After a few days she had hoisted her courage like a shield and asked him to expand on his criticisms. He'd resisted at first, but she'd been relentless. She wanted to know—she had to know—what he'd been getting at before she'd flown into that crying rage.

Glory snuggled deeper into the recollection, picturing in her mind that afternoon when she'd cornered him on the couch. She'd draped herself across him, using the burden of the twins as an extra weapon. Wade had pushed gently at her shoulders, trying to talk sense to her, telling her that he didn't want to hurt her again. It wasn't worth it. He was a lover . . .

". . . not a fighter." His hands brushed down her sides and he froze. "Glory, get up before you hurt yourself. You're pregnant—"

"I know I'm pregnant. I also know that you don't like my book. Now tell me why you don't like it. I'm ready to listen."

"Okay, okay!" He sagged against the couch. "Get up. I can't breathe."

"I'm glad you've finally realized that I can overpower you at will." She removed herself, somewhat awkwardly, from him and sat at the other end of the couch. "Pour us some wine, and let's talk literature."

"This is so stupid," Wade complained as he placed the book he'd been reading on the table and poured wine into two glasses. "I don't know anything about writing— good or bad."

Glory eyed the book he'd just been reading. "Truman Capote." She pointed to the volume. "I'd say you know quite a bit about good literature." She took one of the glasses from him. "What didn't you like about my book?"

Wade stalled. He swirled the red wine in his glass and sniffed its bouquet as if he were a connoisseur. The sight brought a chuckle from Glory. There was something weird about a man who inhaled the fragrant bouquet of wine as it wafted up from a Mickey Mouse glass.

"I didn't think it was you."

His abrupt statement chased away her whimsy and she sat up as straight as the twins would allow.

"What does that mean?"

Wade set down the glass and twisted toward her. "It was as if you were trying to imitate the style of another writer. It wasn't you."

"Who was it?"

"I don't know!" Wade ran the fingers of one hand through his hair, letting it tumble negligently onto his forehead. "It just didn't sound like you."

"Lots of writers imitate their peers."

"Yes, until they find their own style. Actors do it, too. But once you've found your own way of doing things, you stick with it. It works because it's you. This book . . . uh . . . what's it called?"

Glory narrowed her eyes and seethed. *"Talking Heads."*

"Talking Heads has a good story and good characters. The idea of going behind the scenes of an early morning talk/news show is fascinating, and the characters are very real, but the style is awkward. It's as if you're uncomfortable with the telling of the story. When the characters are talking or thinking, it's fine. But when you get into the . . . the . . . what do you call it when the author talks?"

"Narrative."

Wade nodded. "When you get into the narrative, it gets bogged down, as if the author is trying to impress you with the prose instead of just melting into the story." Wade glanced at the ceiling for a few moments. "It's like hearing an actor delivering Hamlet's soliloquy in Brooklynese. It's jarring."

Glory stared at him as lights went off in her head. Heavenly days! He'd hit on it! She felt as if heavy chains had just dropped from her wrists and ankles. She was free. She understood what the critics were complaining about, and she knew exactly how to appease them.

"I don't know what I'm talking about, Glo. It's got to be a good book, or it wouldn't have been published. Let's just forget—"

"You're absolutely right," she interrupted.

"Good. Discussion closed."

"No, no." Glory grasped his forearm. "I mean you're

absolutely right about the problem with the book. I was trying to be someone I'm not. Even Penny said my style had changed, but I took that as a compliment. Penny was trying to nudge me toward the light, but I was determined to stay in the dark."

"I'm right?" He looked dumbfounded.

"Yes!" Glory pulled him toward her and kissed him. "Thank you. It was a painful experience," she admitted with a grin. "Sort of like giving birth, but it was worth it."

"God, I was right!" He was still steeped in amazement. "Maybe I should quit acting and start writing."

Glory tensed slightly but managed a tight smile. "Go right ahead."

He snapped from his shock and held up his hands in surrender. "No thanks. I know it's a lot harder than it looks."

She relaxed. "Just like acting."

Wade curled his fingers under her chin. "Are we partners again?"

"We're partners."

"Good. I'm miserable when we're mad at each other. It breaks my heart." His lips sought hers, sealing his testimony with a kiss, and she listened to the sound of . . .

". . . and I hate to break this up, but dinner is gonna be on the table in thirty minutes!"

Peaches' voice whisked away Glory's lovely digression, and she sat up in the bed, mirroring Wade's own position.

"Okay! Thanks, Peaches." Glory turned to Wade. "Dinner is served, sir."

"Were you sleeping?"

"No."

Wade glowered at her. "Naturally. You stayed awake just to make me feel inadequate, right?"

Glory laughed. "You've got it."

He pushed himself from the bed and stretched his arms over his head, then froze. He pivoted slowly toward her, and his dark brows rose and fell to punctuate his exaggerated words. "I *have* got it."

"What?"

"The urge to ravish your body again!" His accent was straight out of Transylvania.

Glory moved her gaze to that telltale part of his body. "Mmmm, so you do. But Peaches has dinner ready, remember?"

"We'll skip dinner."

"Wade! You asked her to fix an early meal."

"We'll have an early meal later." He reached out for her, laughing as she scrambled from the bed to escape him.

"Okay." Glory pointed toward the door. "You go tell Peaches that we're going to eat later."

"Sure thing. No problem. I'm the boss in this family," Wade grumbled as he went to the door. He paused, his hand on the knob, and glanced over his shoulder. A meek expression bathed his face. "Will you tell her for me?"

Laughter rocked her. Glory leaned against him, weak with giggles. Taking his hand, she pulled him toward the bathroom.

"I have an idea. We'll play slap and tickle in the shower."

Wade's eyebrows lifted, and his eyes sparkled. "That sounds wet and wonderful."

"I thought you'd like the idea."

Wade threw open the shower door and motioned her to precede him. "Step into my office, Miss Jones."

Glory smiled. She loved his sense of humor.

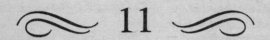 11

TOMORROW'S STARLET FLOATED on her back in the pool. Underwater lights created a halo around her body, which was encased in a gown of silver and navy blue bugle beads. Arms akimbo, her blonde hair so stiffened by hairspray that it repelled water, she wore a serene expression.

"Marla, you're ruining your Bob Mackie original," Fiona Larkin said in a bored tone.

"Oh, well," the floating starlet sighed. "I couldn't wear it again anyway. I mean, it's been seen."

Three photographers crowded at the edge of the pool, their camera flashes popping and motor-drives whirring.

"How nice." Fiona pursed her lips and regarded the photographers with emerald eyes. "Marla's gotten her wish." She whipped her gaze back to the bobbing Blonde. "The photographers are here, darling. They've taken your picture, so you can come out now. Of course you'll look like a drowned rat, but you didn't think about that before you jumped in there, did you?"

A stricken expression erased the serenity on the Blonde's face, and Fiona laughed, a low predatory sound, and made a slow, graceful pivot away from the pool. Glory lingered a moment, watching the Blonde wrestle with her dilemma, then she followed Fiona back into the house where the party raged. Fiona was all aglow in a tight-fitting sheath of ruby red. She parted the crowd of partygoers like Moses parting the waters and headed straight for Wade with Glory in her wake.

"You missed the spectacle, darling," Fiona announced as she squeezed herself between Wade and Tim Simpson, the director, on the two-seat sofa. "Marla was playing lily pad in the pool." Fiona tossed back her blonde hair and laughed. "I hope I never looked that desperate when I was a nobody who wanted to be a somebody." Her eyes collided with Glory. "You didn't stay to watch the finale, dear?"

"No, darling, I've seen the picture before," Glory rejoined, congratulating herself for dipping into the Beverly Hills lingo. "Wade, pick yourself up, dust yourself off, and dance with me." She held out her arms to him.

He grinned, set down his drink, and slipped into her embrace. They two-stepped toward the center of the room, where too many couples danced in too small a space.

"Aren't film-wrapping parties the strangest of all?" he asked close to her ear.

"Absolutely. Who is Marla Range anyway?"

Wade chuckled. "She has a bit part in the film. She plays a waitress with one line of dialogue. Poor kid."

"She knows how to create a splash." Glory wound her arms tighter about his neck and pressed the length of herself to him. "I like your director's taste in houses. Oriental Twelve Oaks, isn't it? Stately columns and magnolia wallpaper mixed with Buddhas and silkscreens."

"He's into Japan, and she's from South Carolina," Wade explained. "He's a good director, though, and she's a gracious hostess."

"I wonder what people say about us?"

"Oh, I don't know. Maybe . . . he's lucky to have her, and she knows it."

"And they make pretty babies together," Glory added with a husky laugh. She inhaled the minty fragrance of his aftershave and spread her fingers into the silken expanse of loose, short curls at the back of his head. "You look good in this suit. It reminds me of Jimmy Cagney and Humphrey Bogart movies." She stepped back a little to examine the double-breasted dark cinnamon jacket. The broad lapels and thin bronze-colored tie added to the illusion of yesteryear, even though she knew he'd bought the outfit only a week ago. She ran her fingers lightly over his off-white shirt, lingering on one of the pearl buttons. "I'm getting ideas."

"Not now!" Wade feigned panic and pulled her back into his arms. "Control yourself, please. I'm trying to make a good impression."

"Why? The film's finished."

"Right, but the check isn't in the mail yet."

"I see your point." She tipped back her head to find his eyes. "Don't look now, but Arnold just joined the party."

"I won't look. I'd rather look at you." He nuzzled the underside of her jaw. "You put every woman in this room to shame."

"I bet you say that to all your wives," Glory teased, but his compliment sent a glow through her. She'd dressed carefully for this occasion, determined to give Fiona a run for her money. The gown of smoky lace was one of her favorites, the one she saved for extra special events. Its tight bodice outlined her breasts and waist. The skirt fell in soft folds. She'd piled her hair on top of her head in painstaking disarray, letting a few tendrils spill to her neck. The only jewelry she wore was her wedding ring.

"Excuse me?" Arnold's hand touched Wade's shoulder. "The song's over, and I've got some news to deliver."

Wade gave Glory a regretful grimace before turning toward Arnold. He slipped his arm about Glory's waist. "First tell Glory how sensational she looks tonight, Arnold."

Arnold regarded her with squinty eyes. "You look very nice, Glory. Very nice."

"Thanks, Arnold." She took in his nondescript black suit. "You're looking fit yourself."

"Thanks." He ran a finger along the inside of his collar. "Wade, let's find a corner. I've gotten word from Farleigh." Arnold's close-set eyes focused on Glory briefly. "You'll be interested in this, Glory. Join us."

"I fully intend to," Glory snapped, then bit her tongue. Why was she always attacking Arnold? Wade never attacked her agent.

They wove through the crowded room and managed to reach the patio doors. Marla wasn't in the pool anymore, and Glory glanced around and spotted her squirming through a space in the hedges. She did look like a wet rat, and she was trying to make a clean escape. Poor thing.

"So what's the word?" Wade grabbed a drink from the tray of a speeding waiter. He looked at it, frowned, and handed it to Glory. "It's a martini."

Glory took the glass from him and grinned. "Better luck next time."

"The word is that you're still going to have to audition for the part and—"

"I already agreed to that," Wade interrupted Arnold.

"Yes, I know." Arnold stuck his hands into his pockets and rocked back and forth on the balls of his feet. "That's never sat easily with me, so I tried to change his mind."

"Arnold, we agreed." Wade grabbed another drink, this time a Manhattan. "Here, you want this?"

"Yeah, thanks." Arnold gulped the drink. "It's a good thing I talked to him, Wade. He told me that you're the only actor he's asking to audition."

"Great!" Glory piped up.

"Not so great." Arnold threw her a chilling glare. "He's willing to consider another actor—no audition necessary—and the guy's only credits are a bit part in an Off-Broadway show and a second lead in the touring company of a musical."

"I don't understand," Glory said, regarding Wade's disappointment and Arnold's biting fury.

"It seems he's leery of Wade's talent. Farleigh doesn't think Wade can cut it on stage." Arnold finished off the drink. "I think it stinks."

Wade heaved a sigh and looked around for another waiter. "Well, I can kind of understand his point. I mean, I haven't proven myself on stage, and the stage is a beast."

"Haven't proven yourself?" Glory stared at him, amazed at his simple-mindedness. "What do you call your work with the Royal Shakespeare Company? What about those Off-Broadway plays you worked in? And what's all this crap about Wade's not being able to cut it? Acting is acting, whether it's done in front of a camera or in front of a live audience. It's not whom you play to, but how you play." A waiter bore down on them, and Glory stepped directly into his path. He skidded to a jarring halt, a fraction of an inch from her. "The star of this extravaganza would like a whiskey and soda."

"Yes, ma'am," the waiter murmured, obviously surprised by her shrill voice. He handed Wade the drink. "Here you are, Mr. Wilson. Can I get you anything else?"

"No, this is fine, thanks."

The waiter stepped carefully around Glory and hurried away. Wade chuckled and shook his head.

"What's gotten into you, Glo?"

"Nothing." Glory strove for a calmer tone. "I just think it's time you used your clout. I mean, you've kissed the likes of Bob Farleigh's feet for years, and it's about time the likes of Bob Farleigh started puckering up to you!"

Wade draped an arm about her shoulders. "Calm down.

So, Arnold, is the audition set?"

"You're not still thinking about auditioning?" Glory pulled away, staring at him in complete amazement.

"Honey, will you calm down?"

"Listen to her, Wade," Arnold spoke up. "She's right. You've got clout now. Use it. I'd like for you to tell me to tell Farleigh that an audition is out of the question under the circumstances. He knows that Bernard is courting you for his next film. Farleigh's putting the screws to you."

"Right!" Glory straightened to her full height. "Arnold's absolutely right. Don't you understand?"

Wade scrutinized her with a sort of speaking vision. "I understand Arnold. I just don't understand you. I thought you wanted me to audition."

"I did, but I don't now."

"I'm not sure I like the song you're singing, Glory." Wade tossed back the rest of his drink, and his eyes narrowed, clearly not entirely from the kick of the liquor. "You were desperate to get me to New York and into that play."

"I know, but—"

'And you never even looked at the script," he interrupted. His voice had a hard edge to it. "You had no idea if it was a good play or a terrible play. You wanted me to take it, sight unseen."

"I—I—" Glory grasped her glass tighter, then gulped at the martini. It was true. She hadn't read the script. She hadn't asked Wade if he thought it was a good play. She hadn't cared one way or the other. It was just a ticket to New York City, where she could reign once more. Shame reddened her cheeks, and she wished Wade would quit looking at her with that penetrating gaze of his.

"What should I tell Farleigh?" Arnold asked, cutting into the uncomfortable silence.

"Tell him to forget it. Set up a meeting with Bernard for me."

Glory's breath escaped in a slow hiss, and she forced herself to smile into Wade's eyes. "Is the Bernard script good?"

"Very good," Wade answered.

"And the Farleigh script?" she ventured.

"So-so. It's not quite up to his usual standards."

Remorse constricted her throat, and not knowing why, she turned pleading eyes to Arnold. Surprisingly he leaped to her rescue.

"Then it's settled! Great!" He craned his neck to peek inside the crowded room. "How about introducing me to your leading lady, Wade? I hear she's having trouble with her agent, and I thought I might talk some business with her."

"I'd be glad to introduce you, Arnold, but speak softly and carry a big stick. She's a barracuda." Wade arched an inquiring brow at Glory.

"I've met her," Glory said with a saucy grin. "I'm going to see if I can find our hostess and thank her for the party."

"Okay, I'll bump into you later."

He strode with Arnold into the house. Glory's mouth twisted as she fought the tears of humiliation. How could she have been so self-centered to encourage him to audition for a play she didn't know anything about other than that brief notice she'd found in *Variety*? Her blurred vision cleared to reveal Maggie Simpson making a beeline for her.

"Here you are!" Her soft drawl worked well with her Scarlett O'Hara gown of mint green. "Wade said you were looking for me."

Glory beheld her round, sweet face and imagined her crooning, "Ashley! Ashley!" Sweeping aside the vision, she took one of Maggie's fine-boned hands within her own. "I just wanted to thank you for hosting the party. Wade and I have enjoyed it."

"Why, you're certainly welcome. I love to give parties. This old house was made for them. I feel as if I know you. Wade talks of you all the time. He's so proud of you." She smiled a Melanie Wilkes smile. "I read your latest best seller, *Touch Me Not*, and I just cried and cried."

"You...cried?" Glory steeled herself. Did this woman hate her book that much?

"I always cry over beautiful things," Maggie explained. "I told my Timmy that it would make such a lovely motion picture. I especially loved the setting." Her dark brown eyes swept upward. "World War II. There's something so romantic about wars and battles." The brown eyes found Glory's again. "The Civil War was the most romantic, even though we lost that one."

Glory told herself not to laugh, but she did anyway. "I'm glad you enjoyed my novel."

"Oh, I did!" Her eyes rounded. "No wonder Wade is always singing your praises."

Glory let Maggie's hand slip from hers. Did this woman have any idea how miserable she was making her? "Well, I don't want to keep you from your other guests. I just wanted to extend my thanks."

"You're welcome, honey. When's your next book coming out?"

"Next year. Probably in the fall."

"I'll be looking for it. You enjoy yourself, you hear?"

"Yes, thank you."

Maggie left her with a swish of taffeta, and Glory turned her back to the sight of the laughing, joking people. She stared into the pool where Marla had baptized herself into the world of infamy. A water bug plopped onto the surface, creating a circle of ripples around its dark brown body. It swam about for a few moments before its wings lifted it back into the air.

Wade's subtle accusation had sent ripples of regret through Glory, and she still felt the disturbance on what had been the calm surface of her self-righteousness. He'd made her take a good, long look at herself, and she didn't like what she saw in the mirror he held. She saw a woman who was afraid of her husband's success, afraid that it would swallow her up and she'd cease to exist. She'd balked at marriage because she couldn't stand the thought of being Mrs. Somebody. Now the threat of being Mrs. Wade Wilson was very real, and it still scared her. She'd fought hard to remain Glory Mathers, never giving any mind to the man who had been labeled Mr. Glory Mathers.

In the early years of her marriage, she'd lovingly nudged Wade toward success, but when fate directed him away from her well-laid plans, she'd retaliated by jerking and pulling him back toward her course, not his. How could she have been so callous to the person who meant everything to her? The person who had always been there to offer advice, support, encouragement?

Lifting her gaze from the pool, Glory watched a fine mist swirl in from the direction of the ocean. Like many of the homes in Beverly Hills, this house was built precariously on a hillside. Beyond the pool, the property ended abruptly, and a shoulder-high, wrought-iron fence discouraged any accidental slips down the steep hill. Lights sparkled in the distance, blurring as the fog rolled in.

The transparent clouds reminded her of that fall in London when she'd spent some of her advance from her second book on a trip there with Wade. They'd left Adam with Wade's parents, and although she hadn't known it at the time, Damon and Dani were blossoming within her. A fond smile curved her mouth. She liked to think that the twins were conceived during that first night in London, about the time Big Ben had struck eleven bells. They'd spent three weeks there and kidded each other about how much they missed Adam.

When they'd returned from London, Glory had dismissed her morning sickness as Great Britain's revenge. A few weeks later she'd glanced at her appointment calendar and gasped. To a woman who was never late for anything, it could mean only one thing—Adam's days as an only child were numbered.

Ropes of mist coiled through the air, and Glory walked around the pool and stood at the filigree fence. Her mind drifted with the fog, sweeping her back to that fall in London when Wade had stood before the Old Vic and gazed at it as a war-weary soldier would his hometown. The fog was heavy that evening . . .

. . . its curling tendrils scurrying along the streets at knee-level. A streetlamp imbued the mist with amber and threw Wade's face into bas-relief against the backdrop of London. He pushed his hands into the pockets of his tweed long-coat. His hair glistened with drops of moisture. His eyes held a hundred memories as he spoke in the quiet murmur of a man addressing himself.

"Oh, I miss her so. She gave me so much self-confidence. I left her to dazzle the world with what she'd taught me." A bitter laugh was tossed into the chilly air. "So much for the spirit of foolish youth."

If she hadn't known better, Glory would have thought he was speaking of an old lover instead of the historical theater. She looped her arm in his, chiding herself for feeling oddly jealous.

"You love the stage, don't you?"

"I love acting." Wade smiled fondly, as if recalling the face of an old friend. "It's like he said, 'All the world's a stage.' It doesn't matter where I act as long as I can act. I'd do a scene from *Hamlet* on top of a double-decker bus if I were given the chance."

"You'll get your chance. There's that Off-Broadway show's audition when we get back to New York."

"Yes, it's a chance." He shifted from one foot to another and hunched his shoulders against a stiff wind. "I'm thinking of changing agents."

"Do you have someone else in mind?"

"You remember that aftershave commercial I did a few months back?"

"Yes." She pressed closer to him, letting him block the bitter wind that gusted now and then.

"There was an agent on the set. He represented the actress who was in the commercial with me. Said his name was Arnold Fletcher, and he wanted to know if I'd ever thought about trying out for films."

"Films?" Glory turned wide green eyes on him. He was still studying the architecture before him.

"He said I was very photogenic and that I was natural before a camera. We talked for a few minutes, and he gave me his card. He impressed me, and my contract with Jim expires at the end of the year. It seems like an omen."

"Does he have any successful clients?"

"I talked to the actress on the set, and she said he represented some of the up-and-comers in the business. She said he might not look like a cagey, fast-talking son-of-a-gun, but that he was and more."

"Well, agents can make all the difference. I had a loser for my first one; she did absolutely nothing for me. I thought I was a washout until Penny came along, and zap! My stuff started selling as fast as I could write it."

"This Fletcher guy said something that stuck in my mind."

"What?"

"He asked if I thought I could handle the demands of filmmaking." A half-smile lifted one corner of his mouth.

"I hadn't ever thought about films as being that demanding on an actor, but maybe they are at that. Then he asked me if I could really act. I told him I could, and he said that was good because he didn't want just another pretty face on his hands. He was looking for actors, not stars."

"He's got some good lines, I'll say that much for him."

Wade looked down at his shoes, as if the sight of the Old Vic had become too much for him. "Let's go find a restaurant."

"I wish I could have seen you perform in there," Glory said as she turned with him and started strolling along the street.

"I wish you could have, too. In fact, I wish we'd known each other years ago. It would have been wonderful if you'd been the first girl I'd made love to."

"I was, wasn't I?"

His eyes touched hers for a startled second, then he laughed. "Yes, you were in a way. You were the first woman I ever held in my arms and felt that frantic rush of love for. The kind that tells a man that he's holding a woman who will take a big piece of him with her if she ever leaves."

Glory leaned her cheek against his shoulder. "You're wonderful when you get all mushy."

He chuckled softly, and his breath escaped in tiny cloud puffs. "London does that to me."

An elderly couple approached them, and Glory and Wade moved to one side to let them pass. The woman wore a long black coat and a hat from bygone days. It had a tattered red plume and a scrap of black veil that shadowed her face. The man wore a shiny blue suit, white shirt, and bow tie. They clung to one another, helping and supporting each other as they picked their way along the pavement through the fog. As they passed, the old woman lost her footing momentarily, and the man's gnarled hands grasped her tighter until she'd regained her balance.

"Steady, love. Don't break me heart," he whispered in a voice that was marbled with age.

"I'm just fine, 'enry, as long you hold onto me."

When they were out of earshot, Wade looked at Glory with amused eyes. "Did you hear that exchange?"

"Yes. I hope we're like that when we're old. Helping each other with each step." She examined the wonder etched on his face. "What is it?"

Wade shook his head briskly. "I don't know. It's just that . . . well, for an instant when I looked at them, I saw us. Years from now." He stopped and turned with Glory. Behind them the fog swirled, but there was no sign of the elderly lovers. "Maybe that *was* us." Wade's voice dipped to a chilling purr. "Maybe this mist is playing tricks on us."

"London does have a strange effect on you," she observed as eeriness invaded her. She looked back at the bulking shape of the Old Vic. "Do you ever wish you'd never left London?"

"Oh, no." He gathered her closer, his arm secure around her waist. "I had to leave here to find you."

"Sometimes I feel as if Adam and I are holding you back. Actors need a certain amount of freedom."

His arm tightened for a moment, and he called up his talent for mimicry. "Steady, love. Don't break me heart. . . ."

". . . Glory? Earth to Glory. Earth to Glory. Respond, please."

Wade's voice broke through the London fog, and Glory stared up into his face for a few moments before London vanished from her mind.

"I'm sorry. I was . . . thinking."

"I'm ready to call it a night. What about you?"

"Yes." Glory glanced toward the house. The room was still jammed with well-dressed bodies. "It's not breaking up yet?"

"No, we'll start the stampede. Here, I've got your shawl and purse." He handed the jeweled bag to her, then draped the lacy triangle across her shoulders. "I've said our good nights to Tim and Maggie."

"Good." She tucked her hand within his and let him lead her around the side of the house to the front, where a uniformed young man stood beside their car.

"Here you go, Mr. Wilson." The young man handed Wade the car keys. "Mr. Wilson?"

"Yes?" Wade opened the passenger door for Glory.

"Could I have your autograph?"

"Sure." He took the proffered pen and paper and scribbled his name on it. "There you go. Good night."

"Thanks ever so much. Good night." The young man leaned down to look at Glory. "Good night, Mrs. Wilson."

"She's Ms. Mathers," Wade corrected with a smile.

"Good night," Glory answered, then settled back in the bucket seat. "Turnabout, fair play."

Wade laughed heartily. "He meant well."

"I know. Thanks for correcting him for me."

"My pleasure."

"And thanks for setting me straight tonight. I guess I needed it."

"No harm intended, Glo." He glanced at her, his face lit by the green light from the dashboard. "We're going to have to discuss this Bernard project."

"Yugoslavia." The word was becoming synonymous with gloom.

"Yes, the filming begins sometime in September."

"During school months," she offered.

"Exactly. There's the rub."

The problem rested heavily between them, creating a tense silence as the Ferrari ripped through the ground fog toward Malibu. Since they'd started sharing each other's lives, they'd never been apart for more than a week at a time, and the prospect of spending months without Wade was nearly unbearable for Glory.

The ocean was in a fit of fury, and Glory watched the giant breakers as the sports car sped through the fog. The house loomed against the cloudy night, and only one light glowed in a downstairs window.

"Looks like everyone's turned in," Wade said as he braked in the driveway. "I'll make a pot of tea, and we can devise a plan of action."

Glory was loathe to discuss the Bernard project, but she knew it had to be dealt with. She switched on a lamp in the living room and turned out the hall light. While Wade put on a kettle of water, she checked on the younger Wilsons. Adam had left the radio on, and she switched it off before tucking the covers around his slim body. She fluffed his hair, noticing that it was exactly the same shade of brown as hers.

Damon murmured in his sleep, and Glory crossed the room to him. He opened one blue eye.

"Mom?"

"Hush. Go back to sleep, baby."

He closed his eye, and his mouth relaxed into a childish pout.

Across the hall, Dani was fast asleep. Her teddy bear was clutched tightly to her chest as if to ward off bad dreams. Glory placed a soft kiss on her daughter's forehead before she tiptoed from the room. Dropping her shawl into a chair, she kicked off her shoes before making her way toward the kitchen area.

"Is it time for tea and sympathy?" she inquired as she eyed the ceramic pot and teacups on the dining table.

Wade ignored her question. "I checked the answering machine for messages. Penny called and said for you to call her back, no matter what time you got in. It must be important."

"What now?" Glory hitched herself onto the kitchen counter and reached for the wall phone. She dialed the number and listened to the static of long distance. "Penny? It's me."

"Oh, Glory!" Penny cleared her throat, and Glory could imagine her levering herself to a sitting position in her huge brass bed. "Good news, hon. Issac Menchum is anxious to talk to you about collaborating on *Touch Me Not* for the stage."

"Issac Menchum?" From the corner of her eye she caught Wade's swift pivot in her direction. "*The* Issac Menchum?"

"Is there any other?" Penny's voice vibrated with excitement. "He loves the book and would like to work on a script with you. He even has some interested backers."

"Oh, my God!" Glory bobbed her head when Wade gripped her arm. "Yes, Wade. Issac Menchum likes *Touch Me Not,* and he wants to work on a stage version with me."

"Outstanding!" Wade planted a wet kiss on her cheek. "Simply outstanding!"

"What, Penny? I didn't catch that."

"Do you have a pencil and paper handy? I have his phone number; he wants you to call him."

"Uh . . ." She glanced around her frantically. "Wade, I need a pencil and a piece of paper."

Wade reached into his jacket and withdrew a pen. "Write it on the wall."

"Okay, Penny. I'm ready." She jotted the numbers

onto the white wall, then wondered if she'd ever be able to remove them. Her hand trembled violently. "Yes, I've got it. I'll call him tomorrow. You'll talk money with him?"

"Yes, later. Just call the man and sweet-talk him. We can't let this fish get away."

"I understand."

"Now what have you decided on that movie deal?"

"Oh, Penny, I can't think about that now."

"Don't play Scarlett O'Hara with me, Glory."

"Put them on ice. If Menchum and I strike a deal, I won't want to be bothered with them."

"It's your career," Penny said in a warning voice. "I wish you'd stop being so narrow-minded. Well, congratulations. I'll be in touch."

"Thanks, Penny. Good night." Glory replaced the receiver and stared at the scribbled numbers on the wall. A heady sense of accomplishment pushed upward. She hadn't felt this way since she'd sold her first book.

"Are you headed for Broadway, lady?"

She snapped herself from her inner ecstasy and grinned at Wade. "Look out, Broadway, here I come."

"Ironic, isn't it?" He placed his hands on her shoulders and tipped his head to one side. "You've spent most of our married life trying to push me toward Broadway, and now you're the one who's headed that way."

His observation stifled her enthusiasm, and she leaned her cheek against his chest.

"Oh, Wade. It isn't quite fair, is it?"

"It's fate, and you can't fight it." He pushed her back a little. "Come on, green eyes. Your tea is ready, but you won't get any sympathy from me."

She slipped from her perch on the counter and sat at the dining table. The tea was cinnamon-flavored, and it soothed her as it went down.

"If I take the Bernard film, it looks as if you and the kids will have to stay here or in New York while I'm in Yugoslavia."

Glory nodded. "It looks that way." Emotion wedged in her throat. "I'll miss you."

"You're not going to start crying, are you?"

She met his eyes and felt hers brim with tears even as she shook her head no.

Wade pushed back his chair and held out his arms. "Come here, Broadway lady. Have a seat."

She sat in his lap, wrapping her arms about his neck and sobbing into his shoulder. His hands patted her as if she were a child.

"Glory, don't cry," he pleaded above her sobs. "I can't stand it when you cry. Why can't you be happy for me? I'm happy for you."

"We're not going to be together," she managed, her voice muffled by his jacket.

His fingers roved through her hair, removing the pins and letting it fall to her shoulders. "We'll always be together. Two months, Glory. That's not a lifetime. It'll pass in a blink of an eye."

"It'll seem like years!"

"Honey, don't make it worse for me than it already is. I need you to be strong."

His words cut off her tears, and she sniffed. She was being a weakling, and she despised that. Raising her head from his soggy shoulder, she wiped away the wetness and streaked mascara from her face.

"I'm okay." She pushed back her hair and drew a deep breath.

"Are you sure?"

"Yes."

"Give us a Glory-ous smile," he commanded, holding her head between his hands. "Come on, just for me, Glo.

You can do it. I see it coming . . . it's almost there . . . watch out . . . watch out . . ."

Her mouth curved against her bidding.

"Ah-ha!" His lips touched hers. "'I can no other answer make but thanks, And thanks,'" he quoted.

Glory smiled. She loved Shakespeare.

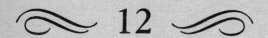 12

CREDITS ROLLED ACROSS the freeze-frame, and music swelled from the speakers mounted on either side of the screen. Glory watched as the names of those responsible for *Twisting Turns* scrolled up the screen, but her mind was still riveted to the performance she'd just witnessed.

"Aren't you glad I invited you?"

Glory looked at the man seated beside her in the private projection room. "Arnold, he's wonderful, isn't he?"

"He's one helluvan actor." Arnold jabbed a pudgy finger toward the screen. "Wade Wilson has given his best performance to date, but I'd wager he'll turn in an even better one in the Bernard film."

The screen blackened, and the lights went up. The voice of the studio's projectionist floated into the room.

"Okay, Mr. Fletcher?"

"Okay. Thanks." Arnold turned around in his seat and waved at the projectionist, whose face appeared behind a square of glass. "I'll treat you to lunch, Glory. We've never done that before. How about it?"

"I never turn down a free lunch, kid." She stood and followed him from the room. Arnold guided her through the catacombs of the studio headquarters, pausing to allow her to gaze in wonder at a ten-foot-tall picture of Wade that graced one wall in the front foyer.

"He's special, or they wouldn't have his picture out here. You're married to a bona fide superstar, Glory."

"I'm beginning to see that, Arnold. It's a little hard to accept." She squinted against the glare of the midday sun. "I'd be more than happy to settle for a hamburger and fries."

Arnold opened the passenger door of his black Mercedes. "I love a woman who has simple tastes."

"Does your wife?"

He waited until he'd slid under the wheel before he answered, "Bella has the simplest of tastes. She thinks I'm extravagant."

"A match made in heaven," Glory observed with a smile. "I am glad you invited me to see the rough cut of Wade's film. He's probably still asleep back home. The poor man is exhausted. He's always so tired after he's completed a film."

"It's grueling work. I don't know how the actors hold up under it." He pulled into the parking lot of a chain restaurant. "Is this okay?"

"My kids love it. They'll be green with envy when I tell them I lunched—free—here."

Arnold smiled, and this time it reached his eyes. "You've got great kids, Glory."

The compliment stunned her, and she eyed him warily as they walked from the car into the restaurant. Arnold guided her toward a booth at the back where he could keep an eye on his Mercedes through the plate-glass windows. They ordered hamburgers, fries, and Cokes.

"Arnold, you puzzle me." Glory cradled her chin in her hands. "I always thought you didn't care much for my kids—or me, for that matter."

"That's not true." He drained a glass of water.

"I always thought you'd breathe a sigh of relief if my marriage crumbled."

Arnold loosened his tie. "Glory, I wouldn't wish that on anyone. I've been through a divorce, and it isn't pretty."

"I didn't know that you'd been divorced."

"Many years ago. I married Bella . . ."—he paused in reflection—"eighteen years ago, I guess. No, Glory. I never hoped that you and Wade would divorce. I just . . . well, I just think that sometimes you mean well, but you push too hard."

"We all have our faults. The pushing comes from loving him so much." She folded her arms on the table and addressed Arnold with a steady gaze. "Don't you think he could succeed on Broadway?"

"No doubt about it." Arnold lapsed into silence while the waitress placed their food before them. "But he's doing fine work here, and he's reaching millions of people."

"The stage was his goal," Glory said, partly to herself.

"*Was* is the correct tense," Arnold noted. "Sometimes destiny leads you away from your goals." He pinned her with eyes that suddenly sparked with excitement. "You should see him at work—really at work, Glory. Directors praise him. Producers beg for him. Other actors hope to work with him. He's not just another actor; he fills the set with pure talent."

Arnold bit into his hamburger and chewed vigorously before he continued, "His earlier films—even the one for which he received a nomination as Best Actor last year—weren't worthy of his talents. *Twisting Turns* is the first script we've gotten that really showcases him. It's going to knock filmgoers on their ears."

Glory stuffed a couple of fries into her mouth and smiled. She enjoyed hearing such empyrean praises about Wade. He deserved every delicious adjective. "He's so good in that film," she said, swallowing the fries. "I forgot it was him after a while. I found myself studying his face and the way he talked as if I'd never seen him before."

Arnold winked slyly. "The sign of good acting when

even his wife forgets who it is up there. Tell Wade that. It'll tickle him."

They devoured their greasy meal and exchanged happy smiles. Glory marvelled that she was actually breaking bread with Arnold Fletcher and enjoying herself. He was really a sweet man underneath all those brusque, boring characteristics of his. Maybe he'd collected those traits to keep the plastic "in" people away from him. Glory studied him with renewed respect. She had to hand it to him: it was a clever way to keep away undesirables. Arnold looked positively yawn-inspiring.

When they'd finished their lunch, Arnold drove her home. He waved at the kids when they stampeded toward the Mercedes.

"Hi, Mr. Fletcher!" Their voices rose above the purr of the engine.

"Hello, kids. Good to see you." He waved again, then drove slowly away from the house.

"Daddy's fixing us lunch, and he said he'd lock us in our rooms if we didn't stay out of the kitchen!" Dani placed her small fists at the waist of her yellow sunsuit.

"Then you'd better stay out of the kitchen, shortie. Where's Peaches?"

"She went grocery shopping and to pick up the dry cleaning," Damon answered.

"Oh. I'll go rescue Daddy." Glory bounded up the steps and threw open the door. "Ricky, I'm home!"

"Babaloo! I'm in the kitchen having a nervous breakdown."

"What's the trouble?" Glory asked, rounding the corner and observing his disgruntled expression. She grinned at the sight of him wearing her red apron with its white-lettered "Pig Out" message across the front.

"The can opener is on the fritz, and I can't get this stupid can of tuna open." He flung the offending can onto the counter and muttered a scathing oath.

"Calm down. Julia Child would be positively ashamed of you." She examined the can opener. "What's wrong with it?"

"It just sits there."

She checked the cord. It was dangling half-in and half-out of the socket. "It's not plugged in, Wade." She pushed it in and tested the appliance. It whirred like a top.

"I don't believe this." Wade dropped onto the high stool near the refrigerator. "This has been a terrible day."

Glory placed a kiss on the tip of his nose. "Poor baby. Mommy will fix it."

He offered a diluted smile. "All the fixings are in that bowl. Just needs the tuna."

"Okay." She opened the can and dumped the contents into the bowl. While she stirred the concoction, she regarded Wade's dark frown. "What are you thinking about?"

"Yugoslavia."

"Does it sound like paradise now?"

"No. I'm having second thoughts about the whole thing."

"What? I thought you'd made up your mind to—"

"I had made up my mind . . . I thought." He stood and waved his arms in an agitated way. "I don't know. I just hate the thought of leaving you and the kids. I mean . . . is the script worth it?"

"I don't know. I haven't read it."

"Will you read it?"

She dropped the spoon into the bowl and turned toward him. "Would you like for me to?"

"Sure. Read it and tell me if you think it's good."

"Okay."

"It's in our bedroom on the night table. You go read it, and I'll give the kids their lunch."

She pushed herself from the counter. "It's all yours."

She hesitated before leaving the kitchen. "Wade, why haven't you ever asked me to read scripts before?"

He reached into a wicker basket and withdrew slices of bread. "You never seemed interested. Every time I mention film scripts, you always get that cornered-animal look on your face." He plopped tuna salad onto each slice of bread. "I'd really like to get your opinion on this one, Glo."

She left him to his tuna salad and went upstairs to their bedroom. Picking up the black-bound script, she stretched out on the bed and began to read it with her critically trained eye.

It was immediately absorbing, sweeping her into its passion and colorful characters. Titled *Enemies Without Faces,* the story centered on a clergyman in Poland at the outbreak of World War I. He was torn between his desire to settle himself and his family in a neutral zone and his duty to stay in his motherland and give spiritual guidance to his people. The dialogue was crisp and realistic, and more than once Glory found herself moved by the story line.

The sun was resting on the horizon when she finished the script. She laid it to one side and mulled over what she'd read. It was a fine piece of work, and she could easily picture Wade in the role of the anguished clergyman. The story had wonderful elements of uncommon valor, blind faith, and boundless devotion.

She was consumed with envy. Could she ever hope to create something for the stage that could compare to this piece of art? It wouldn't be easy, but Menchum would guide her. He'd been so happy when she'd said she'd love to work with him. He'd rained compliments upon her about her work and said he'd been a devout fan since the publication of her first novel. He even liked *Talking Heads.* An amazing man, Menchum.

Wade swung open the bedroom door. "Have you finished yet? Peaches will have dinner on the table in a few minutes."

"I've finished." She sat up in the bed and enjoyed the look of anticipation on his face. He was almost bursting with curiosity.

"Well? What did you think of it?" He sat on the corner of the bed and glanced down at the script.

"I think you should definitely go to Yugoslavia."

His eyes were a bright, startling blue. "You do? You liked the script?"

"It's a wonderful script. I read each word with grudging envy. It's made for you, Wade. You'll do it justice."

He laid his hand on the script, and a wistful smile found its way to his mouth. "It's such a challenge. The character I play has so many dimensions. I've played some real cardboard characters, but this one has a beating heart."

"I went with Arnold today to see the rough cut of *Twisting Turns* at the studio."

His hand jerked atop the script, and his eyes flashed. "What did you think?" He did a double take. "You went with Arnold?"

"Yes," she said with a giggle. "With Arnold. And I loved every minute of it." She covered his hand with hers. "Oh, Wade! You're so talented. It gives me shivers just to think about it. I sat in that small projection room and stared up at this . . . this stranger. He looked like you, but he wasn't you. He was a man married to a woman who raced cars. He wasn't the guy who sleeps with me every night. It was such a weird feeling, but it felt good." She curled her fingers around his. "Arnold is right. You shine up there on the screen. Hollywood seems to have embraced you . . ."

"And?" He turned his hand over and laced his fingers with hers.

Glory took a deep breath and decided it was time to

face her fears. "And I'm afraid of it all, Wade."

"Tell me, Glo."

"I'm afraid that our relationship won't be able to withstand separations. I'm afraid I'll become Mrs. Wade Wilson. I'm afraid your career will swallow mine. I'm afraid of Tinsel Town. Most of all, I'm afraid of losing you."

"And all this time I thought you were a tough lady." His voice was tender.

Glory shook her head, and her hair fell forward to hide her frightened expression from him. "I'm not so tough. I used to be before you came into my life and became so important to my everyday existence. I knew you'd eventually work your way into my system so that the very thought of losing you would be totally unbearable. It's happened." She pulled her lower lip between her teeth and waited for a few moments for her voice to steady. "Lately I've been frantic. I've been thinking about us—all the steps we took to become us—and I've been clinging to the past because the future seemed so uncertain."

A movement in the doorway stopped the flow of Glory's erupting confession, and she focused teary eyes on Peaches.

"Dinner's ready." Peaches glanced at Wade and then back to Glory. "I'll feed the kids and put the rest in the oven for you to eat later." She smiled knowingly and closed the door.

"See, Wade? She's not so bad."

"No, she's not." He curled his fingers under her chin and lifted her gaze to his. "And our future isn't so bad either." Abruptly he stood and went to the window. Dusk was moving across the ocean. "I'm not crazy about Los Angeles. I've told you that. But California is a big state, and I'm sure there's a perfect place for us here. Someplace where the kids can get a good education and make friends. Someplace that won't claw at our New York upbringing and try to rip us to shreds. All we have to do is look for that place.

"As for us," he turned from the window to regard her with serious eyes, "we're as constant as that ocean out there. Separations, quarrels, disappointments, career conflicts—whatever—can't destroy us. You're as tough as I am, Glory. If I could handle being Mr. Glory Mathers, you can handle being Mrs. Wade Wilson. Besides, I can't imagine your putting up with that for very long." He smiled and stuck his hands in the back pockets of his jeans. "My career could never swallow yours unless you allow it to. You're right, I'm talented. But so are you. Nothing keeps you from that typewriter, Glory Mathers. After more than ten years of living with you, I can attest to that."

"Yes, but—"

"Let me finish." He sat beside her on the bed and pulled her into the crook of his arm. "Didn't you finish a novel while you were practically in labor with the twins? Didn't you threaten not to attend the Academy Awards banquet with me unless I left you alone to write? Didn't you put in three hours a day at the typewriter when you were queasy with morning sickness? My God, Glory! I've seen you edit copy while you nursed Adam! And you think my little career is going to destroy that drive of yours? No way."

The telephone shrilled and then stopped ringing as Peaches picked it up somewhere in another part of the house. Wade kissed the back of Glory's ear and then ran the tip of his tongue along the side of her neck.

"Any questions?"

"Hollywood is tough on married people," Glory ventured, still feeling a touch of insecurity.

"We won't live in Hollywood. Films and Hollywood don't necessarily go together. And we'll always keep our place in New York. We'll be bicoastal. That has a nice ring, doesn't it?"

Knuckles rapped against the door.

"Yes, Peaches?" Wade asked.

"Your mother's on the phone, Mister Wade. You want me to tell her to call back later?"

"No, I'll talk to her." He sighed and lifted his arm from Glory's shoulders. "I should speak to her. The poor thing probably thinks I'm avoiding her."

"Yes, go on."

He glanced at the telephone near the bed. "I'll take it downstairs. You stay in here and think about what I've said. Think hard, Glo." He bounded off the bed and strode from the room.

Glory lay back and closed her eyes. When had she fallen so madly in love with him? Had there been one particular moment? She searched her memory but couldn't find anything adequate. It was strange the way a person could weave himself into the fabric of another person's life. She'd fought commitment to him, knowing that he was that missing thread that would complete her tapestry so perfectly that she'd never be able to yank him out without destroying everything in the process. Even when she'd stood before a minister and vowed to love Wade forever, she had told herself that she could live without him. Perhaps at that moment she could have, but not now. Life without Wade would be like New York without literati. No attraction.

Suddenly she remembered the first time the full impact of her love for Wade Wilson had slammed into her. It had been a stormy, indigo night, and Wade had been at the studio filming *Tie-Breaker*. They were living in that bungalow in Beverly Hills, and Wade had told her he'd be home no later than eight o'clock. She'd eaten dinner, played with the kids, then put them to bed. At nine-thirty, she'd called the studio. Wade had left at seven.

The panic! She remembered it so well. That clammy, throat-tightening panic. At ten she'd called the director, but he didn't know where Wade could be—he'd left the studio at seven and had said he was going home. At ten-thirty she'd called Arnold. He hadn't heard from Wade. At eleven she'd phoned Lila St. Claire, his co-star. Wade? He wasn't home? No, she hadn't seen him since he left the studio, and that had been . . .

". . . hours ago. You must be frantic."

"I am. If you hear from him, will you phone me?"

"Of course. Glory, just calm down. He'll be home any minute."

"Yes, okay. Thanks, Lila. Sorry to bother you."

"No bother."

Glory replaced the receiver and stared out the window. Sheets of rain beat against the glass, and trees swayed and tossed their heads like wild, leafy stallions. Should she call the police? She closed her eyes, then opened them again when a vision bounced into her mind—Wade pinned in a crumpled car on the side of the road some-where. He's dead.

"No, no!" She buried her face in her hands and tried to keep the terrible thoughts from crowding into her mind like ghostly demons. "Wade, please come home. Please, come home! Oh, God, I love him so much. Don't take him from me."

As if in answer to her frantic prayer, she heard a car door slam. She lifted her tear-stained face, and a sob tore at her throat when she saw Wade running up the steps to the front door. The door popped open, and he stepped inside and shook himself like some great shaggy dog.

"Lucy, I'm ho—What's wrong?"

"What's wrong? What's wrong?" Her voice climbed toward its upper register. "It's midnight! I thought you were dead." She balled her hands and flew at him, her fists landing solid blows on his wet slicker. "Don't you ever do that to me again! Ever!"

His fingers wrapped around her wrists. "Glory, I'm sorry. I went with some of the crew for a couple of drinks, and I lost track of time."

"Don't you speak to me!" She wrenched from him and stumbled blindly across the room. Sinking onto the sofa, she gave in to her hysteria.

"Glory, don't cry." He sat beside her and brushed his hand through her hair.

"Don't touch me! Look what you've done to me. I'll never forgive you. Never, never, never." She curled into a ball, turning her back to him.

"What have I done to you? Okay, I should have phoned. Take it easy. I'm here now, and everything's all right."

"It's not all right, damn you!" She glared at him, hating him for reducing her to a whimpering, frightened female. "I love you!"

Bewilderment bathed his face, and he laughed softly. "Well, then? Well, then?"

Angry words died in her throat. Blue eyes sparkled at her in the dimly lit room, and she'd never seen such a lovely sight in her whole life. She collapsed into his arms, rubbing her cheek against his wet slicker and thanking everything good in the world for giving him back to her.

"I love you, Glory. Am I forgiven?"

"Yes," she sighed. "For now . . ."

". . . are you asleep?"

"No." Glory opened her eyes to Wade. "I was thinking as ordered."

"Good. What do you think?" He resumed his position on the bed, pulling her into his arms, pressing the back of her head to his chest.

"I think I love you very much."

"And that chases away all your fears?"

"No, but it puts them into perspective."

His arms tightened around her. "You're my touch-stone, Glory. Nothing comes before you and the kids. If things get too complicated, too trying, we'll regroup and take a different course."

"Together?"

"Always together. Always."

She rolled onto her side, sliding her hands up his chest. "How's your mother?"

"Fine. She sends you her love." He kissed her hair. "By the way, Peaches took the kids to a movie."

"Darling Peaches."

"We'll give her a raise. She deserves it."

"Good, then she can enroll in some writing classes."

"Writing classes?" He sighed. "Glory, you're not still egging her on, are you?"

"She's interested in writing. She was before she met me."

"So now I have to live with two writers?"

She looked up at him. "You're complaining?"

"No, ma'am. I love writers. Especially the female kind with green eyes and brown hair and soft, full breasts." His hands covered her, and his thumbs moved across her blouse where her nipples strained for closer contact.

Glory smiled. She loved his taste in women.

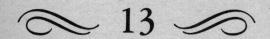

13

IT HAD BEEN a hectic three weeks, and Glory was feeling the impact. Packing and moving back to New York, entertaining Wade's parents, helping him plan his trip to Yugoslavia, getting the kids into school, setting up her work schedule with Issac Menchum; all of it had left her weak, and she was living on pure adrenaline.

The noisy bustle at the airport wasn't helping her frayed nerves. She glanced toward the tight group of people standing a discreet distance from her and Wade. The minister and the saint would be leaving tomorrow— thank goodness. They'd flown in from their retirement home in upstate Virginia ten days ago to visit before Wade headed for his location shoot. Howard and Edna Mathers were chattering away, and Wade's parents looked a bit befuddled. Peaches and the kids stood to one side. Adam and Damon were playing hopscotch on the checkerboard carpeting, and Dani was crying. Dani didn't like good-byes.

"This is it, I guess."

Glory gazed up into Wade's cloudy blue eyes. "I miss you already."

He dropped his carry-on case to the floor, and his arms held her fast. "I'll phone you every week."

Running her fingers through his hair, Glory fought back her tears. "Twice a week, maybe? We can afford it."

"Three times a week," he said with a chuckle. "We're going on a second honeymoon when I get back. You can pick the spot."

"A second honeymoon?" She smoothed his dark hair from his forehead. "That sounds wonderful. I'll work hard and have the play ready for you to read when you get back."

"You want me to read it?" That wonderful brow lifted.

"I've decided that I should take advantage of my association with you. Who would know better than an actor if a play works or not?"

"Menchum might have something to say on that subject."

"I've already discussed it with him. He thinks it's a fabulous idea. He's a big fan of yours."

The small talk dwindled, and Glory's throat tightened. Other passengers were heading for the long tunnel attached to the waiting airplane. She closed her eyes as Wade bent his head. His lips lingered on hers, reluctant to part company.

"I'll write you some love poems while I'm away," he murmured against her mouth. "I won't even mind if you edit them."

"I won't edit them. I'll treasure them." Her lips melted into his. The tip of her tongue raced across his teeth before he opened his mouth to receive her. Tears ran unheeded down her cheeks, and she was surprised to see glistening moisture in Wade's eyes when the kiss ended.

He cleared his throat and retrieved his carry-on. Looking past her, he waved to his parents and blew a kiss to his children.

"Do good work, sweetheart," Glory whispered, her fingertips caressing the tiny dimple in his chin.

"I will." His eyes held hers for a few moments. "See you in two months, Glo."

"Take care of yourself, Wilson. You belong to me."

He clutched the carry-on and walked to the security desk. Passing through the electronic monitor, he glanced over his shoulder and mouthed, "I love you."

Glory dabbed at the tears on her cheeks and turned toward the rest of her family. She went to Dani and hoisted her into her arms.

"Don't cry, baby. Daddy will be back soon."

"Why does he have to go?" Dani asked in a high-pitched voice.

"He has to go to work."

"But why can't we go with him?"

"Because we have things to do here—like going to school and writing plays and books." She kissed her daughter's wet cheek. "He'll be back in no time."

"Mom, can we have quarters to play Gobble-Man?" Adam asked, pointing toward a row of flashing machines.

"No, we're going home." She smiled at her parents and in-laws. "Why don't you all come back to the apartment, and Peaches and I will whip up something to eat."

"Don't mind if we do," Howard answered.

Glory led the way, walking briskly along the corridor with Dani in her arms and her sons hopping from one square to another.

"Are you okay?" Peaches asked, eyeing her with concern.

"I'm fine. Just fine." Glory thought of the promised second honeymoon and the work that awaited her. The play, her next novel, a possible screenplay. There was so much to do in the next two months. But she'd have the time. With the kids in school and Wade in Yugoslavia, she could devote long uninterrupted hours to her writing. And there was that second honeymoon trip to look forward to as a reward for her hard work.

Looking forward. It had been some time since she'd done that. Maybe she was finally through with clinging to her past as a drowning person would a life raft. Suddenly her future was much more interesting than her past.

"There's Daddy, Mommy!" Dani pointed to a framed poster of Wade. It was an advertisement for *Miami Sundown*.

Glory stopped before it and examined the dark-haired, blue-eyed man with the rakish grin. Her husband.

She smiled. She loved Wade Wilson.

DON'T MISS THESE TITLES
IN THE
SECOND CHANCE AT LOVE SERIES

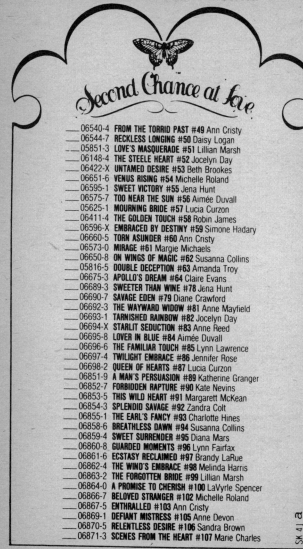

____06872-1 **SPRING FEVER #108** Simone Hadary
____06873-X **IN THE ARMS OF A STRANGER #109** Deborah Joyce
____06874-8 **TAKEN BY STORM #110** Kay Robbins
____06899-3 **THE ARDENT PROTECTOR #111** Amanda Kent
____07200-1 **A LASTING TREASURE #112** Cally Hughes $1.95
____07203-6 **COME WINTER'S END #115** Claire Evans $1.95
____07212-5 **SONG FOR A LIFETIME #124** Mary Haskell $1.95
____07213-3 **HIDDEN DREAMS #125** Johanna Phillips $1.95
____07214-1 **LONGING UNVEILED #126** Meredith Kingston $1.95
____07215-X **JADE TIDE #127** Jena Hunt $1.95
____07216-8 **THE MARRYING KIND #128** Jocelyn Day $1.95
____07217-6 **CONQUERING EMBRACE #129** Ariel Tierney $1.95
____07218-4 **ELUSIVE DAWN #130** Kay Robbins $1.95
____07219-2 **ON WINGS OF PASSION #131** Beth Brookes $1.95
____07220-6 **WITH NO REGRETS #132** Nuria Wood $1.95
____07221-4 **CHERISHED MOMENTS #133** Sarah Ashley $1.95
____07222-2 **PARISIAN NIGHTS #134** Susanna Collins $1.95
____07233-0 **GOLDEN ILLUSIONS #135** Sarah Crewe $1.95
____07224-9 **ENTWINED DESTINIES #136** Rachel Wayne $1.95
____07225-7 **TEMPTATION'S KISS #137** Sandra Brown $1.95
____07226-5 **SOUTHERN PLEASURES #138** Daisy Logan $1.95
____07227-3 **FORBIDDEN MELODY #139** Nicola Andrews $1.95
____07228-1 **INNOCENT SEDUCTION #140** Cally Hughes $1.95
____07229-X **SEASON OF DESIRE #141** Jan Mathews $1.95
____07230-3 **HEARTS DIVIDED #142** Francine Rivers $1.95
____07231-1 **A SPLENDID OBSESSION #143** Francesca Sinclaire $1.95
____07232-X **REACH FOR TOMORROW #144** Mary Haskell $1.95
____07233-8 **CLAIMED BY RAPTURE #145** Marie Charles $1.95
____07234-6 **A TASTE FOR LOVING #146** Frances Davies $1.95
____07235-4 **PROUD POSSESSION #147** Jena Hunt $1.95
____07236-2 **SILKEN TREMORS #148** Sybil LeGrand $1.95
____07237-0 **A DARING PROPOSITION #149** Jeanne Grant $1.95
____07238-9 **ISLAND FIRES #150** Jocelyn Day $1.95
____07239-7 **MOONLIGHT ON THE BAY #151** Maggie Peck $1.95
____07240-0 **ONCE MORE WITH FEELING #152** Melinda Harris $1.95
____07241-9 **INTIMATE SCOUNDRELS #153** Cathy Thacker $1.95

All of the above titles are $1.75 per copy, except where noted

---

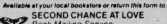

Available at your local bookstore or return this form to:

SECOND CHANCE AT LOVE
Book Mailing Service
P.O. Box 690, Rockville Centre, NY 11571

Please send me the titles checked above. I enclose _____
Include $1.00 **for postage and handling if one book is ordered, 50¢ per book for two or more. California, Illinois, New York and Tennessee residents please add sales tax.**

NAME _____

ADDRESS _____

CITY _____ STATE/ZIP _____
(allow six weeks for delivery)

SK-41b